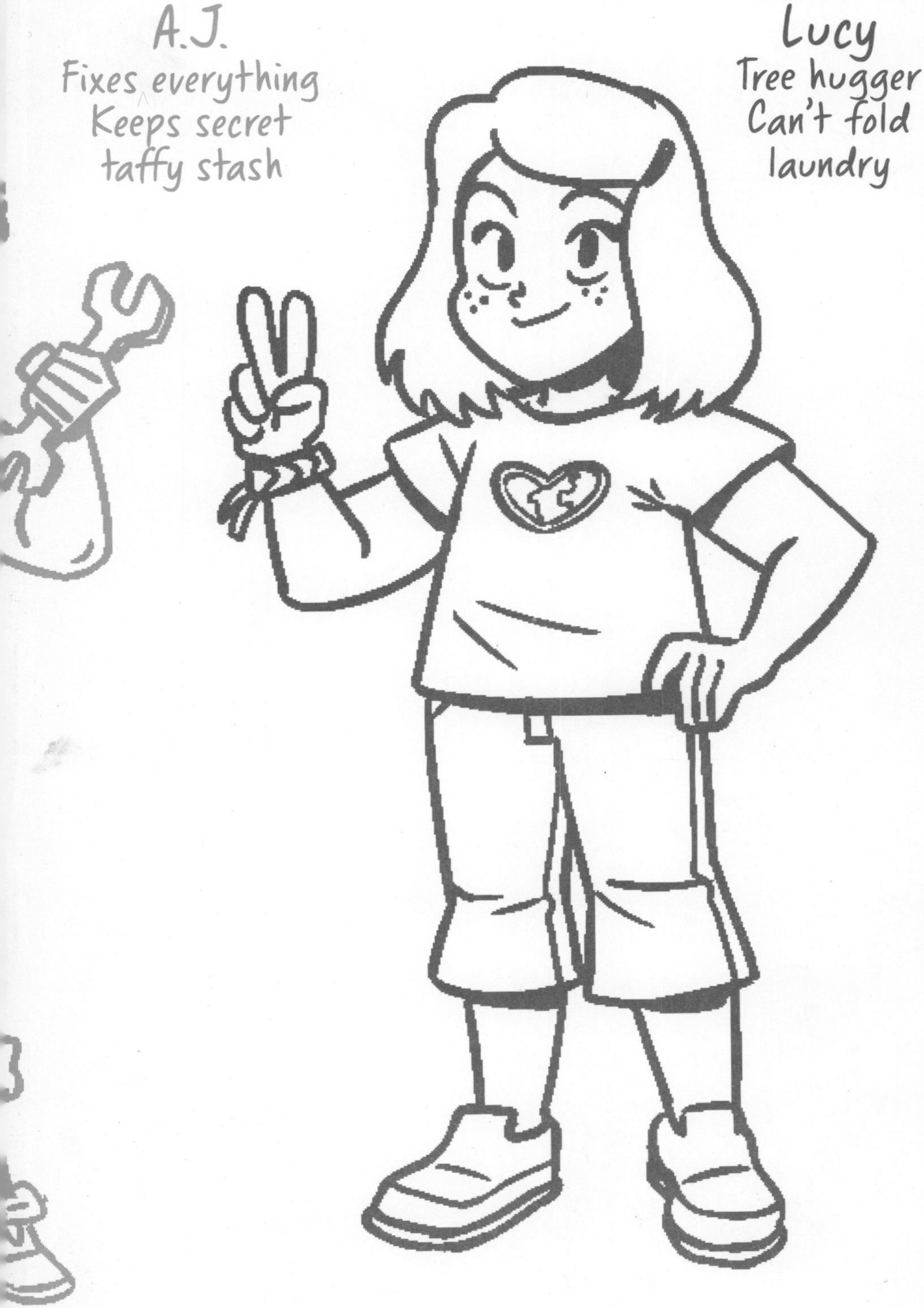
A.J.
Fixes everything
Keeps secret taffy stash
Lucy
Tree hugger
Can't fold laundry

MORE GREAT GRAPHIC NOVEL SERIES AVAILABLE FROM PAPERCUTZ™

THE SMURFS #21   **THE GARFIELD SHOW #6**   **BARBIE #1**   **THE SISTERS #1**   **TROLLS #1**

GERONIMO STILTON #17   **THEA STILTON #6**   **SEA CREATURES #1**   **DINOSAUR EXPLORERS #1**   **SCARLETT**

ANNE OF GREEN BAGELS #1   **DRACULA MARRIES FRANKENSTEIN!**   **THE RED SHOES**   **THE LITTLE MERMAID**   **FUZZY BASEBALL**

HOTEL TRANSYLVANIA #1   **THE LOUD HOUSE #1**   **MANOSAURS #1**   **THE ONLY LIVING BOY #5**   **GUMBY #1**

geeky f@b 5 ™

#1 "It's Not Rocket Science"

LUCY & LIZ LAREAU—Writers
RYAN JAMPOLE—Artist

PAPERCUTZ

NEW YORK

geeky f@b 5

#1 "It's Not Rocket Science"

LUCY & LIZ LAREAU–Writers
RYAN JAMPOLE–Artist
MATT HERMS–Colorist
WILSON RAMOS–Letterer
MANOSAUR MARTIN–Production
JEFF WHITMAN–Assistant Managing Editor
JIM SALICRUP
Editor-in-Chief

© 2018 Geeky Fab Five, Inc. All Rights Reserved.
All other material © 2018 Papercutz.

ISBN: 978-1-54580-122-2

Printed in the China
August 2018

Papercutz books may be purchased for business or promotional use.
For information on bulk purchases, please contact Macmillan Corporate
and Premium Sales Department at (800) 221-7945 x5442.

Distributed by Macmillan
First Printing

Chapter One: First Day. New School.

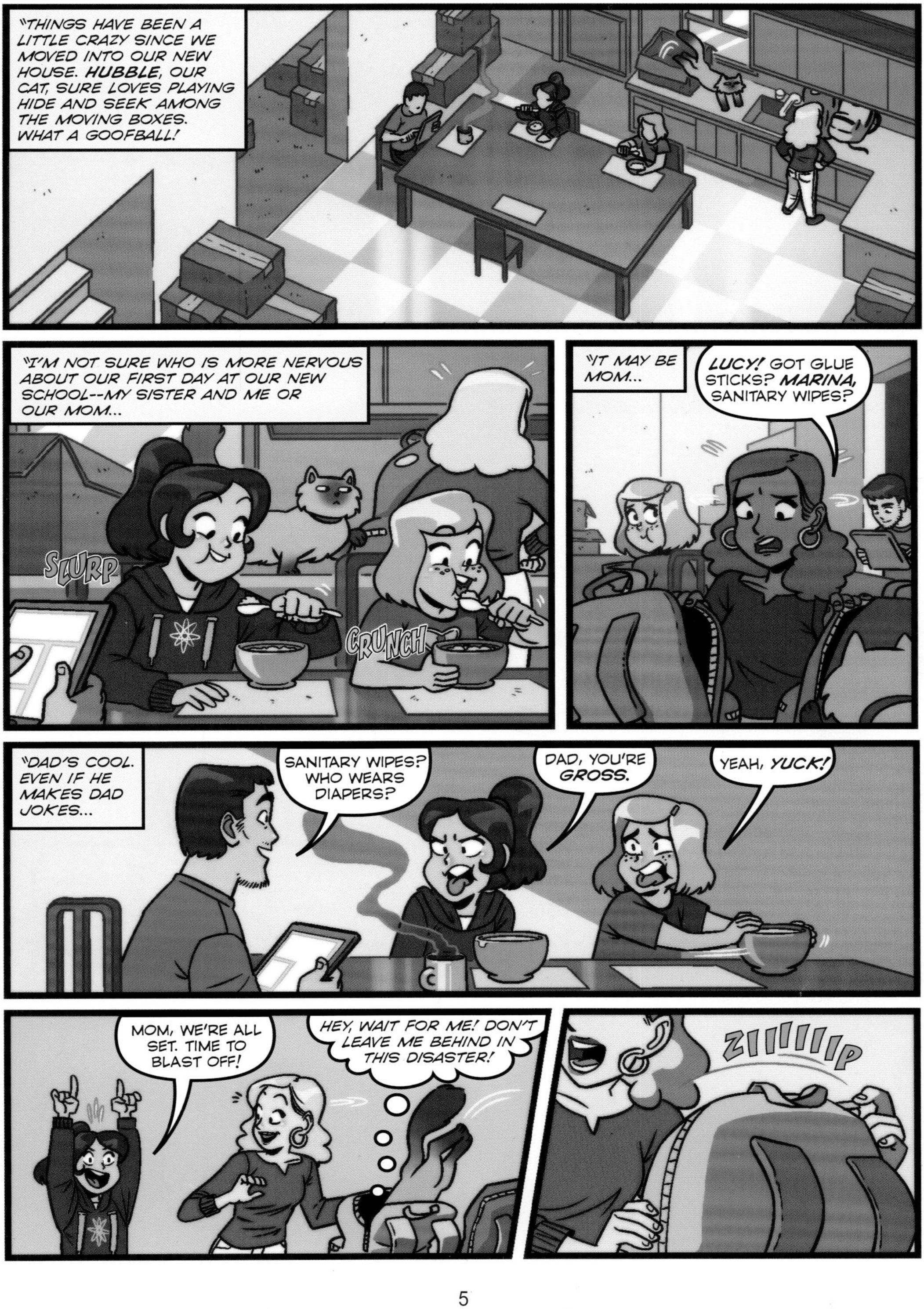
"THINGS HAVE BEEN A LITTLE CRAZY SINCE WE MOVED INTO OUR NEW HOUSE. HUBBLE, OUR CAT, SURE LOVES PLAYING HIDE AND SEEK AMONG THE MOVING BOXES. WHAT A GOOFBALL!
"I'M NOT SURE WHO IS MORE NERVOUS ABOUT OUR FIRST DAY AT OUR NEW SCHOOL--MY SISTER AND ME OR OUR MOM...
SLURP
CRUNCH
"IT MAY BE MOM...
LUCY! GOT GLUE STICKS? MARINA, SANITARY WIPES?
"DAD'S COOL. EVEN IF HE MAKES DAD JOKES...
SANITARY WIPES? WHO WEARS DIAPERS?
DAD, YOU'RE GROSS.
YEAH, YUCK!
MOM, WE'RE ALL SET. TIME TO BLAST OFF!
HEY, WAIT FOR ME! DON'T LEAVE ME BEHIND IN THIS DISASTER!
ZIIIIIIP

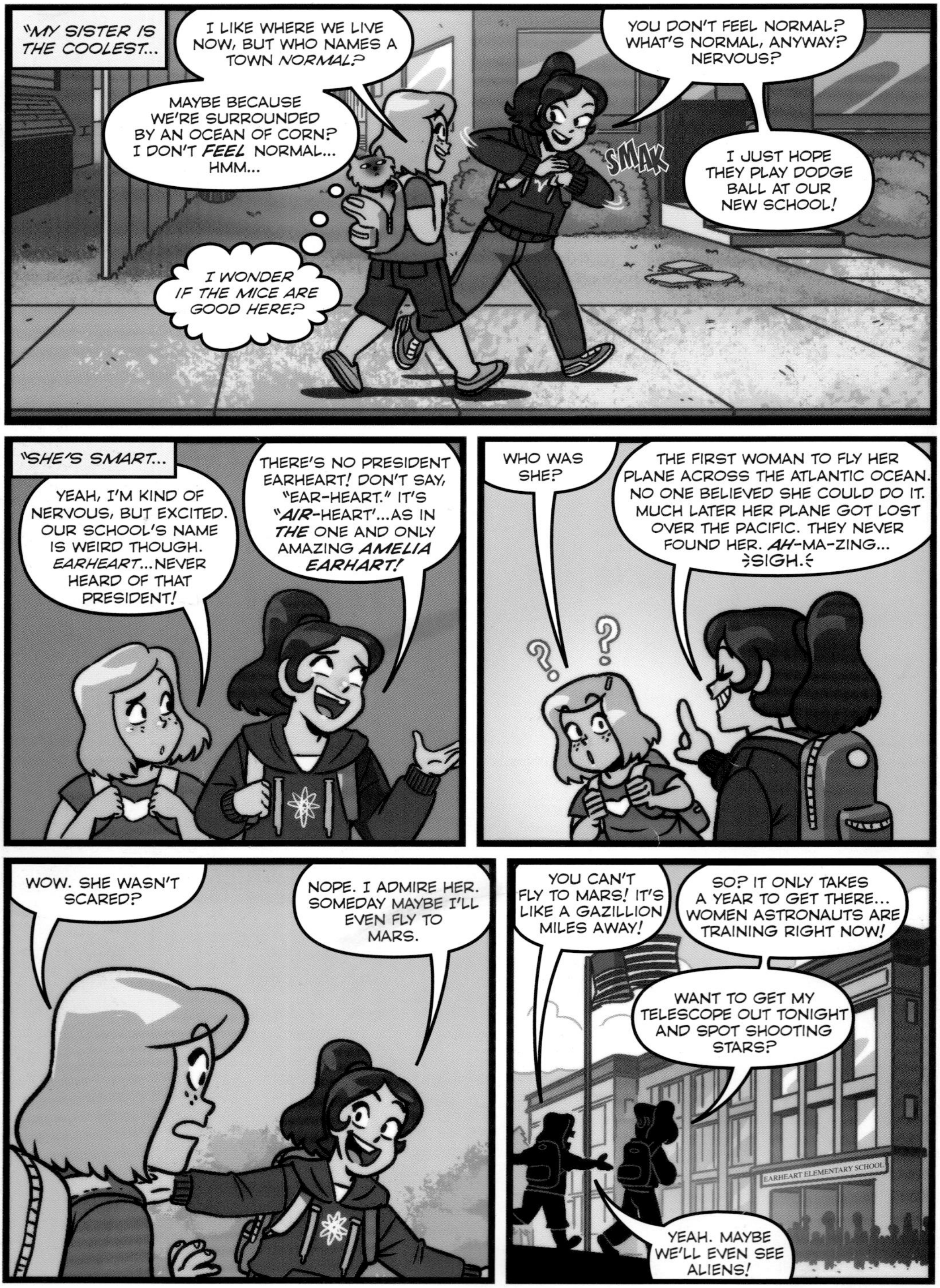
"MY SISTER IS THE COOLEST...
I LIKE WHERE WE LIVE NOW, BUT WHO NAMES A TOWN NORMAL?
MAYBE BECAUSE WE'RE SURROUNDED BY AN OCEAN OF CORN? I DON'T FEEL NORMAL... HMM...
I WONDER IF THE MICE ARE GOOD HERE?
YOU DON'T FEEL NORMAL? WHAT'S NORMAL, ANYWAY? NERVOUS?
SMAK
I JUST HOPE THEY PLAY DODGE BALL AT OUR NEW SCHOOL!
"SHE'S SMART...
YEAH, I'M KIND OF NERVOUS, BUT EXCITED. OUR SCHOOL'S NAME IS WEIRD THOUGH. EARHEART...NEVER HEARD OF THAT PRESIDENT!
THERE'S NO PRESIDENT EARHEART! DON'T SAY, "EAR-HEART." IT'S "AIR-HEART"...AS IN THE ONE AND ONLY AMAZING AMELIA EARHART!
WHO WAS SHE?
THE FIRST WOMAN TO FLY HER PLANE ACROSS THE ATLANTIC OCEAN. NO ONE BELIEVED SHE COULD DO IT. MUCH LATER HER PLANE GOT LOST OVER THE PACIFIC. THEY NEVER FOUND HER. AH-MA-ZING... SIGH.
WOW. SHE WASN'T SCARED?
NOPE. I ADMIRE HER. SOMEDAY MAYBE I'LL EVEN FLY TO MARS.
YOU CAN'T FLY TO MARS! IT'S LIKE A GAZILLION MILES AWAY!
SO? IT ONLY TAKES A YEAR TO GET THERE... WOMEN ASTRONAUTS ARE TRAINING RIGHT NOW!
WANT TO GET MY TELESCOPE OUT TONIGHT AND SPOT SHOOTING STARS?
EARHEART ELEMENTARY SCHOOL
YEAH. MAYBE WE'LL EVEN SEE ALIENS!

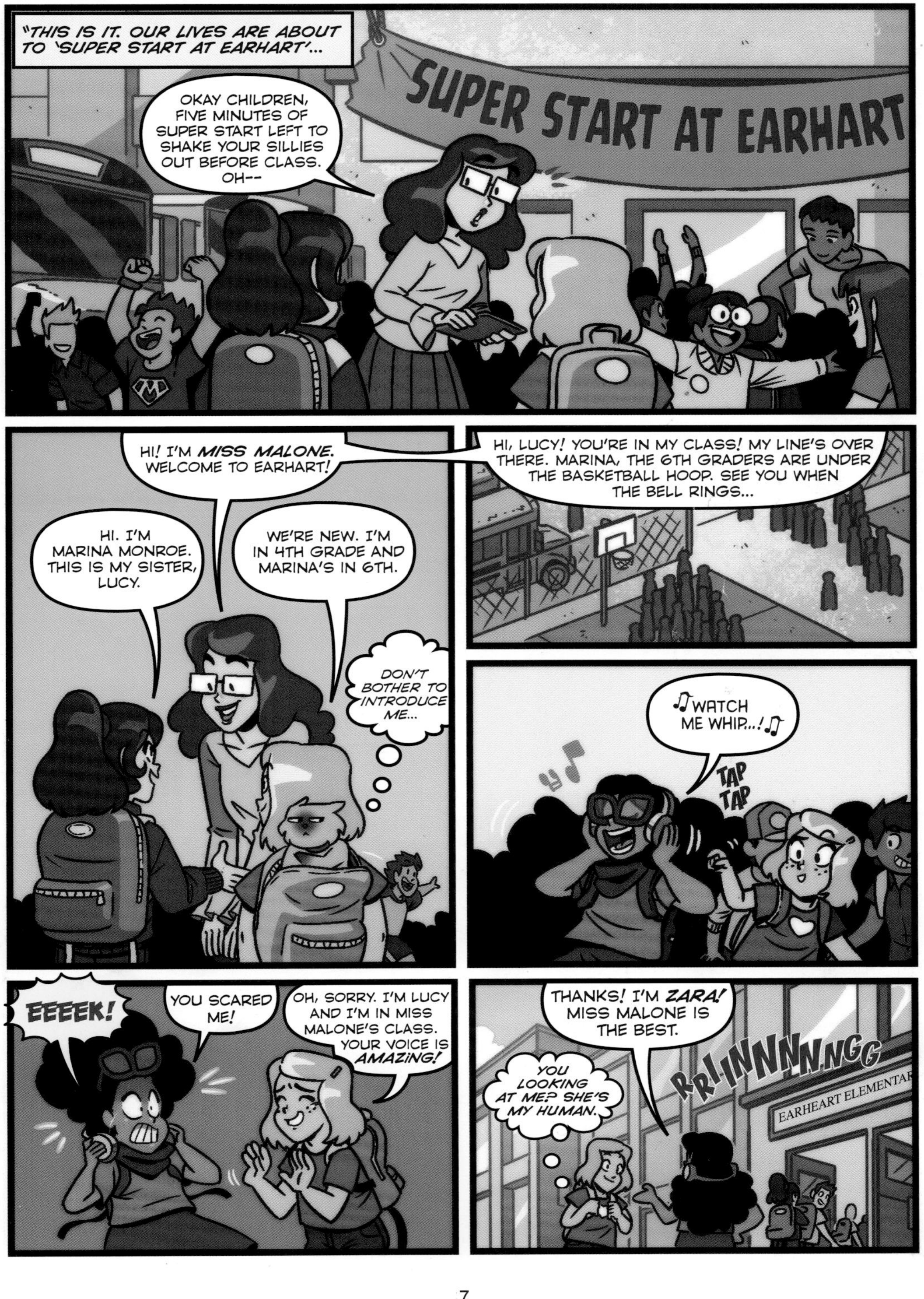
"THIS IS IT. OUR LIVES ARE ABOUT TO 'SUPER START AT EARHART'...
SUPER START AT EARHART
OKAY CHILDREN, FIVE MINUTES OF SUPER START LEFT TO SHAKE YOUR SILLIES OUT BEFORE CLASS. OH--
HI! I'M MISS MALONE. WELCOME TO EARHART!
HI. I'M MARINA MONROE. THIS IS MY SISTER, LUCY.
WE'RE NEW. I'M IN 4TH GRADE AND MARINA'S IN 6TH.
DON'T BOTHER TO INTRODUCE ME...
HI, LUCY! YOU'RE IN MY CLASS! MY LINE'S OVER THERE. MARINA, THE 6TH GRADERS ARE UNDER THE BASKETBALL HOOP. SEE YOU WHEN THE BELL RINGS...
♫WATCH ME WHIP...!♫
TAP TAP
EEEEK!
YOU SCARED ME!
OH, SORRY. I'M LUCY AND I'M IN MISS MALONE'S CLASS. YOUR VOICE IS AMAZING!
THANKS! I'M ZARA! MISS MALONE IS THE BEST.
YOU LOOKING AT ME? SHE'S MY HUMAN.
RRIINNNNNNGG
EARHEART ELEMENTAR

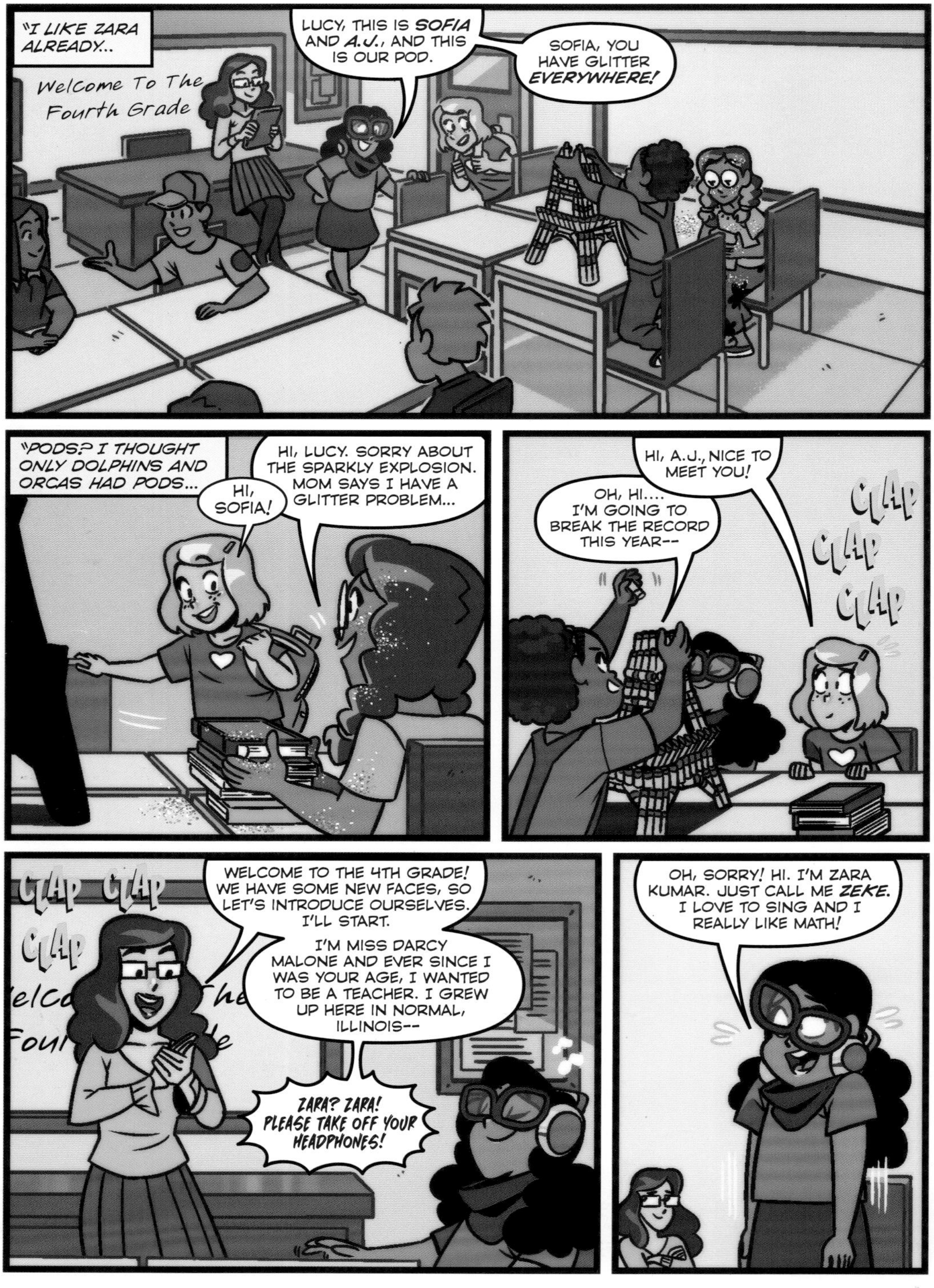

"I LIKE ZARA ALREADY...
Welcome To The Fourth Grade
LUCY, THIS IS SOFIA AND A.J., AND THIS IS OUR POD.
SOFIA, YOU HAVE GLITTER EVERYWHERE!
"PODS? I THOUGHT ONLY DOLPHINS AND ORCAS HAD PODS...
HI, SOFIA!
HI, LUCY. SORRY ABOUT THE SPARKLY EXPLOSION. MOM SAYS I HAVE A GLITTER PROBLEM...
HI, A.J., NICE TO MEET YOU!
OH, HI.... I'M GOING TO BREAK THE RECORD THIS YEAR--
CLAP CLAP CLAP
CLAP CLAP CLAP
WELCOME TO THE 4TH GRADE! WE HAVE SOME NEW FACES, SO LET'S INTRODUCE OURSELVES. I'LL START.
I'M MISS DARCY MALONE AND EVER SINCE I WAS YOUR AGE, I WANTED TO BE A TEACHER. I GREW UP HERE IN NORMAL, ILLINOIS--
ZARA? ZARA! PLEASE TAKE OFF YOUR HEADPHONES!
OH, SORRY! HI. I'M ZARA KUMAR. JUST CALL ME ZEKE. I LOVE TO SING AND I REALLY LIKE MATH!

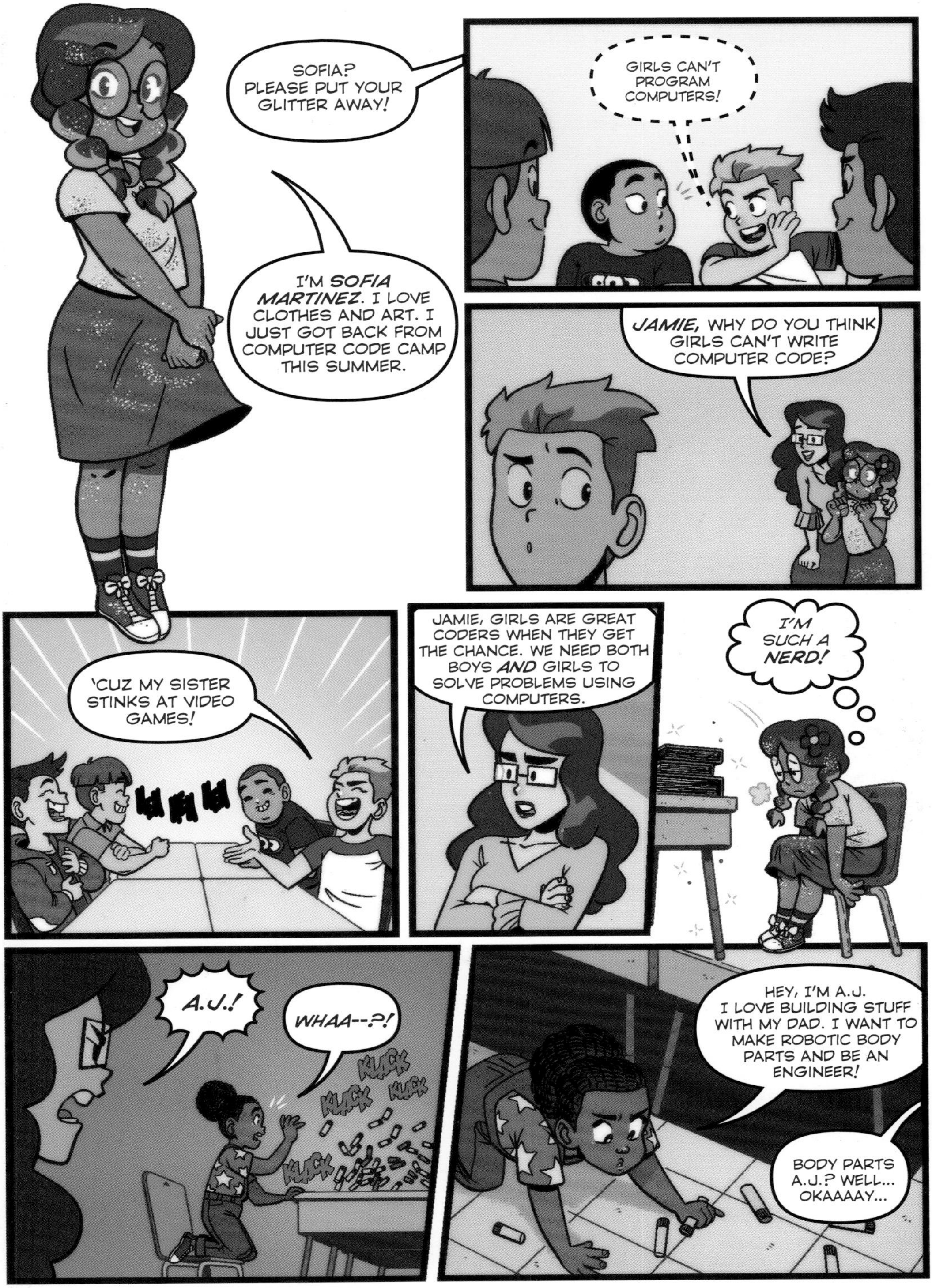
SOFIA? PLEASE PUT YOUR GLITTER AWAY!
GIRLS CAN'T PROGRAM COMPUTERS!
I'M SOFIA MARTINEZ. I LOVE CLOTHES AND ART. I JUST GOT BACK FROM COMPUTER CODE CAMP THIS SUMMER.
JAMIE, WHY DO YOU THINK GIRLS CAN'T WRITE COMPUTER CODE?
'CUZ MY SISTER STINKS AT VIDEO GAMES!
HA HA HA
JAMIE, GIRLS ARE GREAT CODERS WHEN THEY GET THE CHANCE. WE NEED BOTH BOYS AND GIRLS TO SOLVE PROBLEMS USING COMPUTERS.
I'M SUCH A NERD!
A.J.!
WHAA--?!
KLACK KLACK KLACK KLACK
HEY, I'M A.J. I LOVE BUILDING STUFF WITH MY DAD. I WANT TO MAKE ROBOTIC BODY PARTS AND BE AN ENGINEER!
BODY PARTS A.J.? WELL... OKAAAAY...

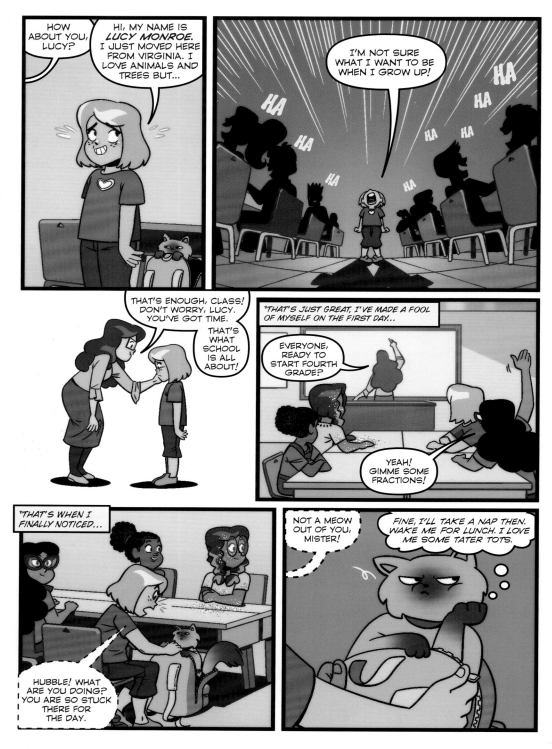

HOW ABOUT YOU, LUCY?

HI, MY NAME IS *LUCY MONROE.* I JUST MOVED HERE FROM VIRGINIA. I LOVE ANIMALS AND TREES BUT...

I'M NOT SURE WHAT I WANT TO BE WHEN I GROW UP!

HA HA HA HA HA HA HA HA HA

THAT'S ENOUGH, CLASS! DON'T WORRY, LUCY. YOU'VE GOT TIME.

THAT'S WHAT SCHOOL IS ALL ABOUT!

"THAT'S JUST GREAT, I'VE MADE A FOOL OF MYSELF ON THE FIRST DAY...

EVERYONE, READY TO START FOURTH GRADE?

YEAH! GIMME SOME FRACTIONS!

"THAT'S WHEN I FINALLY NOTICED...

HUBBLE! WHAT ARE YOU DOING? YOU ARE SO STUCK THERE FOR THE DAY.

NOT A MEOW OUT OF YOU, MISTER!

FINE, I'LL TAKE A NAP THEN. WAKE ME FOR LUNCH. I LOVE ME SOME TATER TOTS.

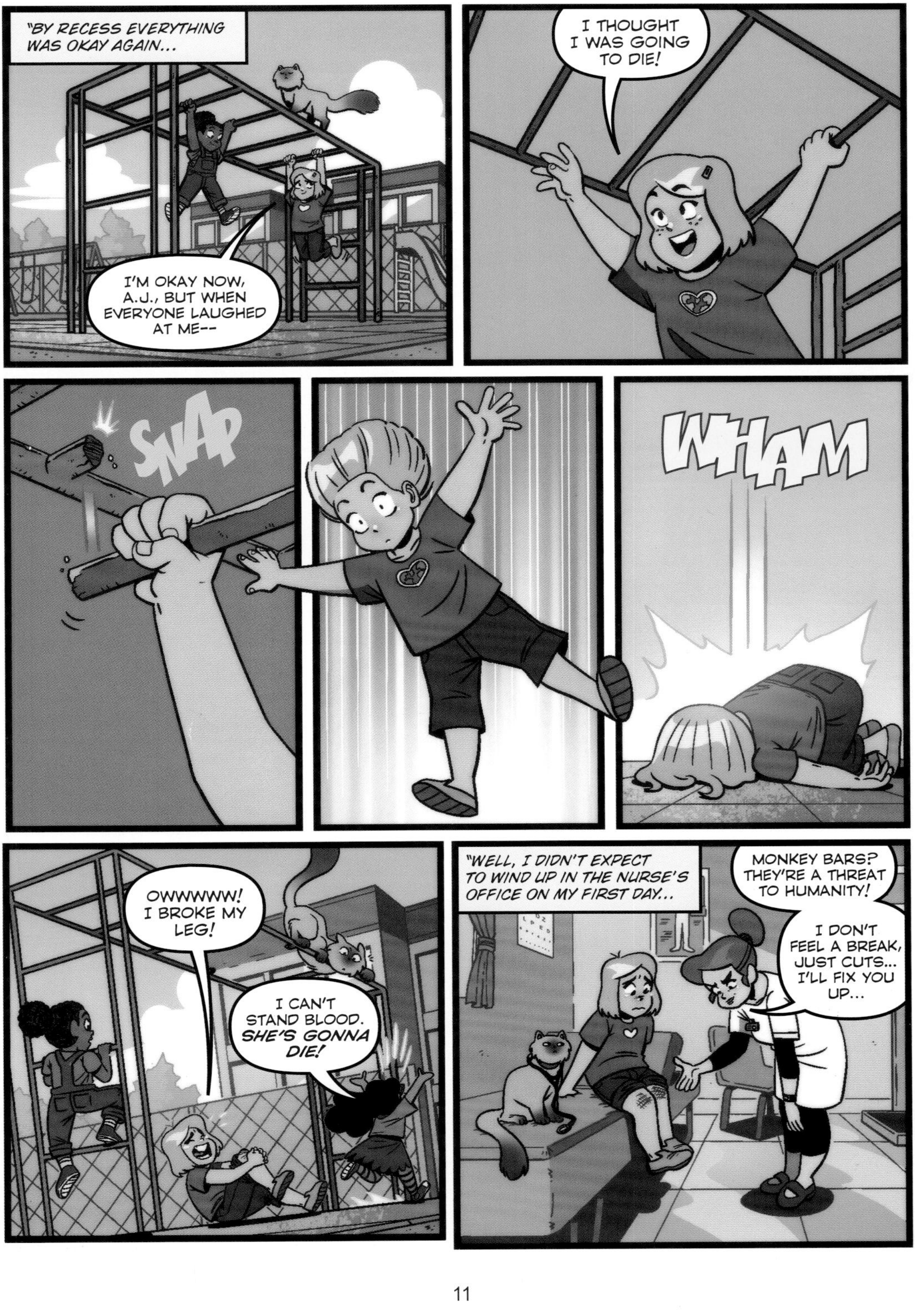
"BY RECESS EVERYTHING WAS OKAY AGAIN...
I'M OKAY NOW, A.J., BUT WHEN EVERYONE LAUGHED AT ME--
I THOUGHT I WAS GOING TO DIE!
SNAP
WHAM
OWWWWW! I BROKE MY LEG!
I CAN'T STAND BLOOD. SHE'S GONNA DIE!
"WELL, I DIDN'T EXPECT TO WIND UP IN THE NURSE'S OFFICE ON MY FIRST DAY...
MONKEY BARS? THEY'RE A THREAT TO HUMANITY!
I DON'T FEEL A BREAK, JUST CUTS... I'LL FIX YOU UP...

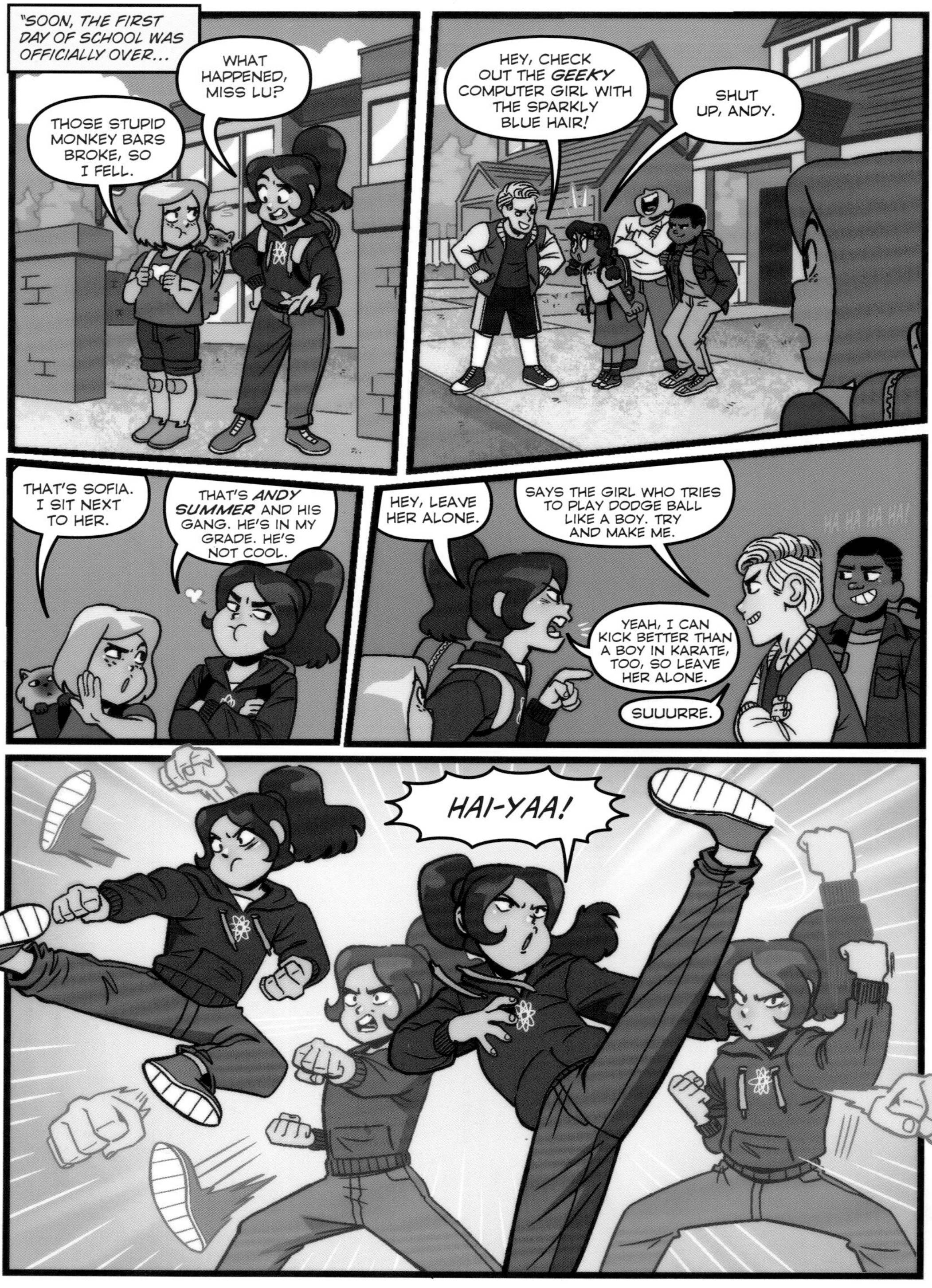
"SOON, THE FIRST DAY OF SCHOOL WAS OFFICIALLY OVER...
WHAT HAPPENED, MISS LU?
THOSE STUPID MONKEY BARS BROKE, SO I FELL.
HEY, CHECK OUT THE GEEKY COMPUTER GIRL WITH THE SPARKLY BLUE HAIR!
SHUT UP, ANDY.
THAT'S SOFIA. I SIT NEXT TO HER.
THAT'S ANDY SUMMER AND HIS GANG. HE'S IN MY GRADE. HE'S NOT COOL.
HEY, LEAVE HER ALONE.
SAYS THE GIRL WHO TRIES TO PLAY DODGE BALL LIKE A BOY. TRY AND MAKE ME.
HA HA HA HA!
YEAH, I CAN KICK BETTER THAN A BOY IN KARATE, TOO, SO LEAVE HER ALONE.
SUUURRE.
HAI-YAA!

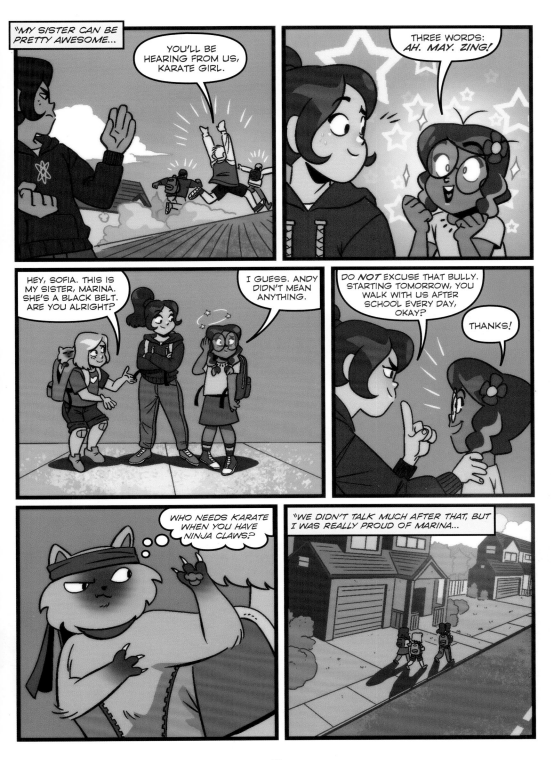

"MY SISTER CAN BE PRETTY AWESOME...

YOU'LL BE HEARING FROM US, KARATE GIRL.

THREE WORDS: AH. MAY. ZING!

HEY, SOFIA. THIS IS MY SISTER, MARINA. SHE'S A BLACK BELT. ARE YOU ALRIGHT?

I GUESS. ANDY DIDN'T MEAN ANYTHING.

DO NOT EXCUSE THAT BULLY. STARTING TOMORROW, YOU WALK WITH US AFTER SCHOOL EVERY DAY, OKAY?

THANKS!

WHO NEEDS KARATE WHEN YOU HAVE NINJA CLAWS?

"WE DIDN'T TALK MUCH AFTER THAT, BUT I WAS REALLY PROUD OF MARINA...

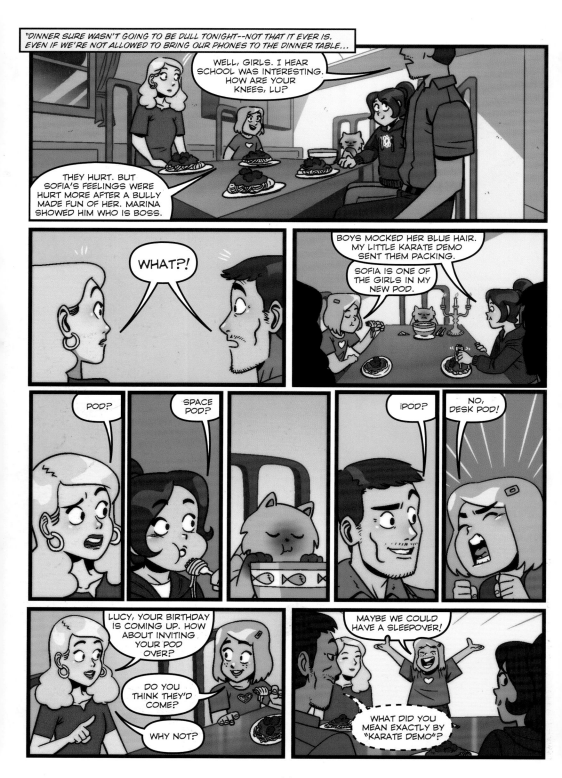

"DINNER SURE WASN'T GOING TO BE DULL TONIGHT--NOT THAT IT EVER IS. EVEN IF WE'RE NOT ALLOWED TO BRING OUR PHONES TO THE DINNER TABLE..."

WELL, GIRLS. I HEAR SCHOOL WAS INTERESTING. HOW ARE YOUR KNEES, LU?

THEY HURT. BUT SOFIA'S FEELINGS WERE HURT MORE AFTER A BULLY MADE FUN OF HER. MARINA SHOWED HIM WHO IS BOSS.

WHAT?!

BOYS MOCKED HER BLUE HAIR. MY LITTLE KARATE DEMO SENT THEM PACKING.

SOFIA IS ONE OF THE GIRLS IN MY NEW POD.

POD?

SPACE POD?

iPOD?

NO, DESK POD!

LUCY, YOUR BIRTHDAY IS COMING UP. HOW ABOUT INVITING YOUR POD OVER?

DO YOU THINK THEY'D COME?

WHY NOT?

MAYBE WE COULD HAVE A SLEEPOVER!

WHAT DID YOU MEAN EXACTLY BY "KARATE DEMO"?

14

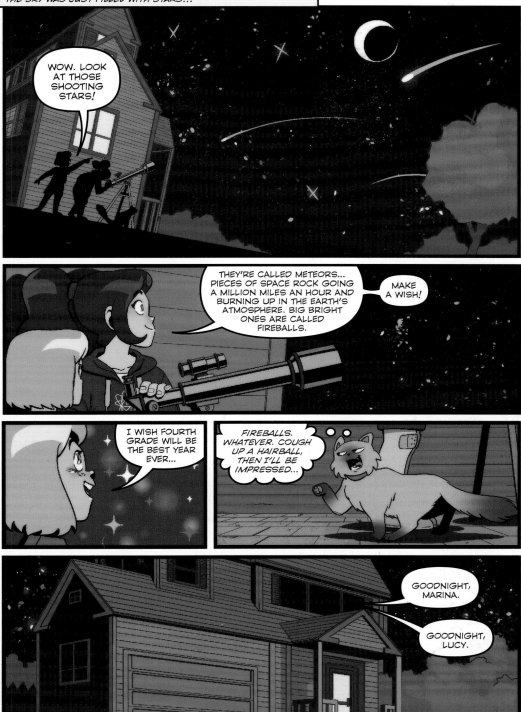

"AFTER DINNER, MARINA, HUBBLE, AND I DID A LITTLE STAR-GAZING.
THE SKY WAS JUST FILLED WITH STARS...

WOW. LOOK AT THOSE SHOOTING STARS!

THEY'RE CALLED METEORS... PIECES OF SPACE ROCK GOING A MILLION MILES AN HOUR AND BURNING UP IN THE EARTH'S ATMOSPHERE. BIG BRIGHT ONES ARE CALLED FIREBALLS.

MAKE A WISH!

I WISH FOURTH GRADE WILL BE THE BEST YEAR EVER...

FIREBALLS. WHATEVER. COUGH UP A HAIRBALL, THEN I'LL BE IMPRESSED...

GOODNIGHT, MARINA.

GOODNIGHT, LUCY.

15

CHAPTER TWO: BYE-BYE PLAYGROUND

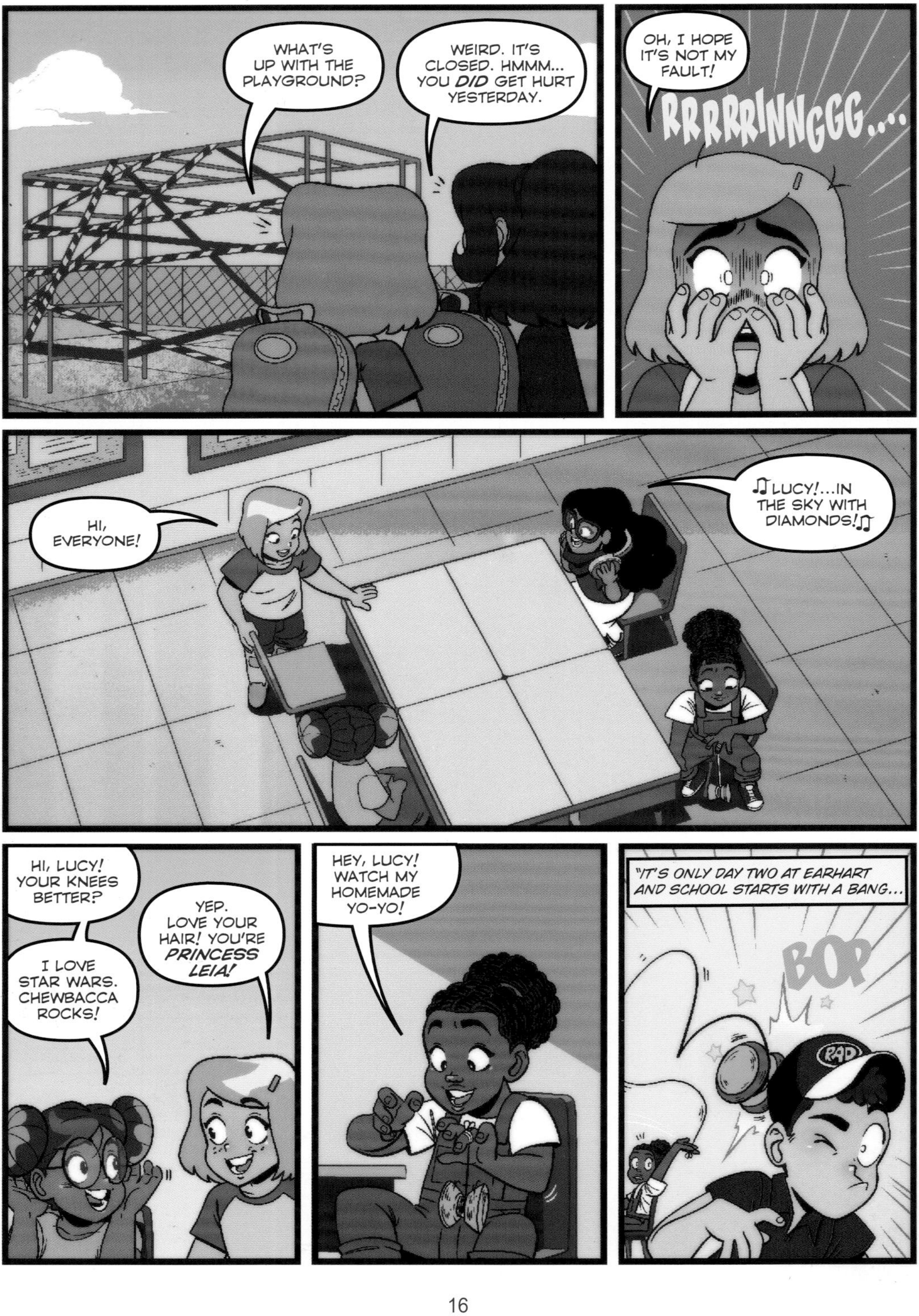
WHAT'S UP WITH THE PLAYGROUND?
WEIRD. IT'S CLOSED. HMMM... YOU *DID* GET HURT YESTERDAY.
OH, I HOPE IT'S NOT MY FAULT!
RRRRRINNGGG....
HI, EVERYONE!
♫LUCY!...IN THE SKY WITH DIAMONDS!♫
HI, LUCY! YOUR KNEES BETTER?
I LOVE STAR WARS. CHEWBACCA ROCKS!
YEP. LOVE YOUR HAIR! YOU'RE *PRINCESS LEIA!*
HEY, LUCY! WATCH MY HOMEMADE YO-YO!
"IT'S ONLY DAY TWO AT EARHART AND SCHOOL STARTS WITH A BANG...
BOP
RAD

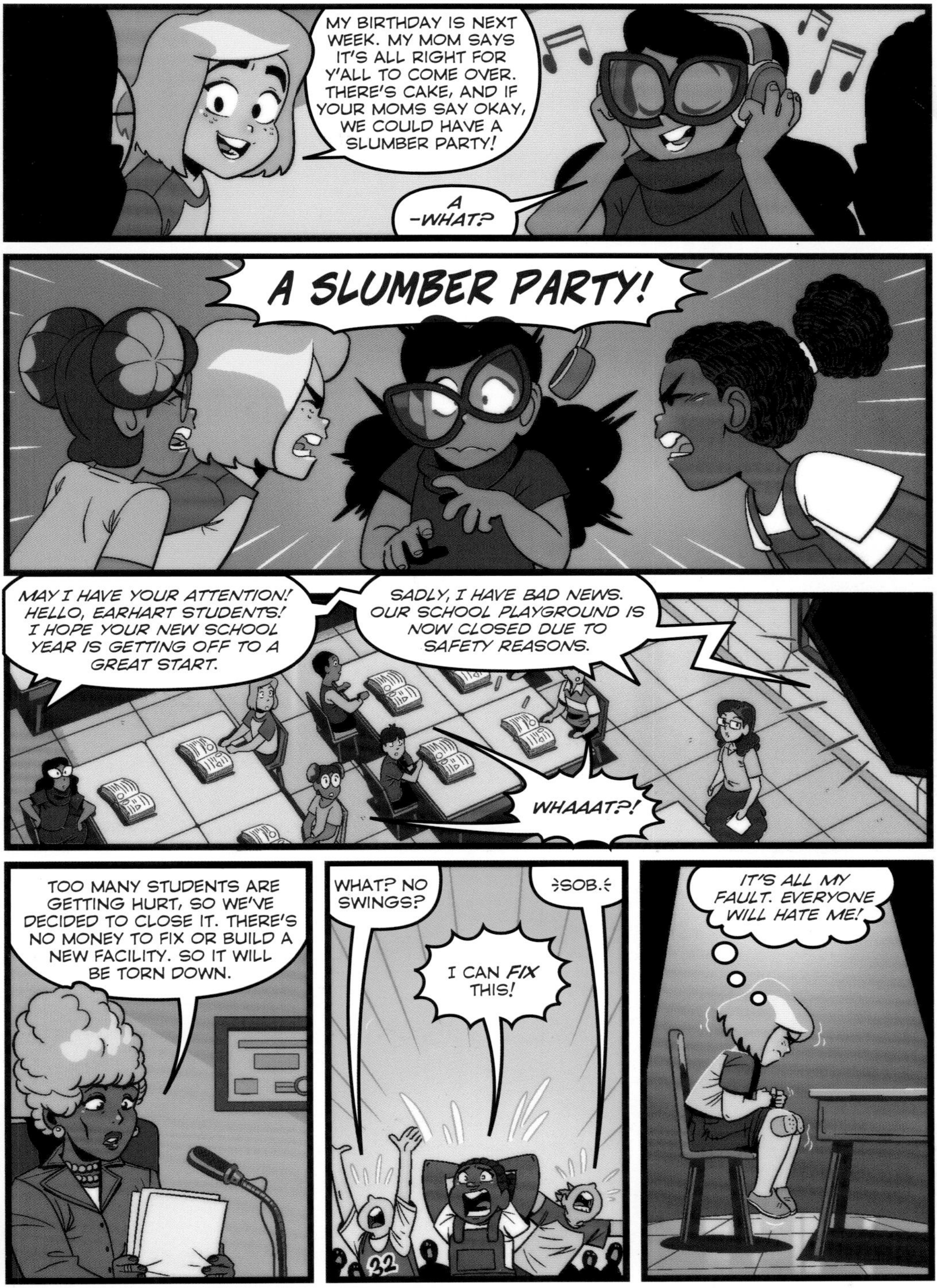

MY BIRTHDAY IS NEXT WEEK. MY MOM SAYS IT'S ALL RIGHT FOR Y'ALL TO COME OVER. THERE'S CAKE, AND IF YOUR MOMS SAY OKAY, WE COULD HAVE A SLUMBER PARTY!
A -WHAT?
A SLUMBER PARTY!
MAY I HAVE YOUR ATTENTION! HELLO, EARHART STUDENTS! I HOPE YOUR NEW SCHOOL YEAR IS GETTING OFF TO A GREAT START.
SADLY, I HAVE BAD NEWS. OUR SCHOOL PLAYGROUND IS NOW CLOSED DUE TO SAFETY REASONS.
WHAAAT?!
TOO MANY STUDENTS ARE GETTING HURT, SO WE'VE DECIDED TO CLOSE IT. THERE'S NO MONEY TO FIX OR BUILD A NEW FACILITY. SO IT WILL BE TORN DOWN.
WHAT? NO SWINGS?
SOB.
I CAN FIX THIS!
IT'S ALL MY FAULT. EVERYONE WILL HATE ME!

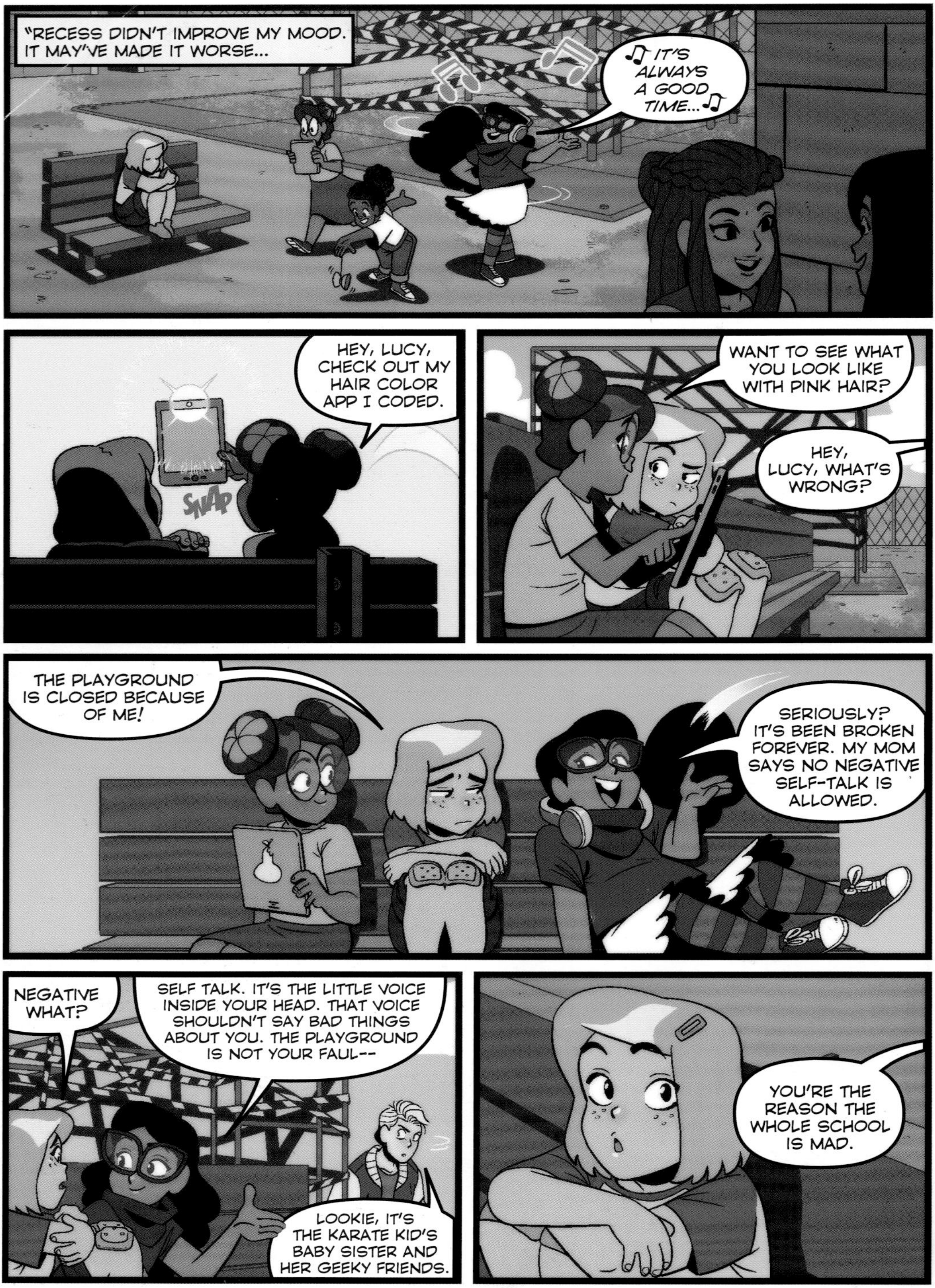
"RECESS DIDN'T IMPROVE MY MOOD. IT MAY'VE MADE IT WORSE...
IT'S ALWAYS A GOOD TIME...
HEY, LUCY, CHECK OUT MY HAIR COLOR APP I CODED.
SNAP
WANT TO SEE WHAT YOU LOOK LIKE WITH PINK HAIR?
HEY, LUCY, WHAT'S WRONG?
THE PLAYGROUND IS CLOSED BECAUSE OF ME!
SERIOUSLY? IT'S BEEN BROKEN FOREVER. MY MOM SAYS NO NEGATIVE SELF-TALK IS ALLOWED.
NEGATIVE WHAT?
SELF TALK. IT'S THE LITTLE VOICE INSIDE YOUR HEAD. THAT VOICE SHOULDN'T SAY BAD THINGS ABOUT YOU. THE PLAYGROUND IS NOT YOUR FAUL--
LOOKIE, IT'S THE KARATE KID'S BABY SISTER AND HER GEEKY FRIENDS.
YOU'RE THE REASON THE WHOLE SCHOOL IS MAD.

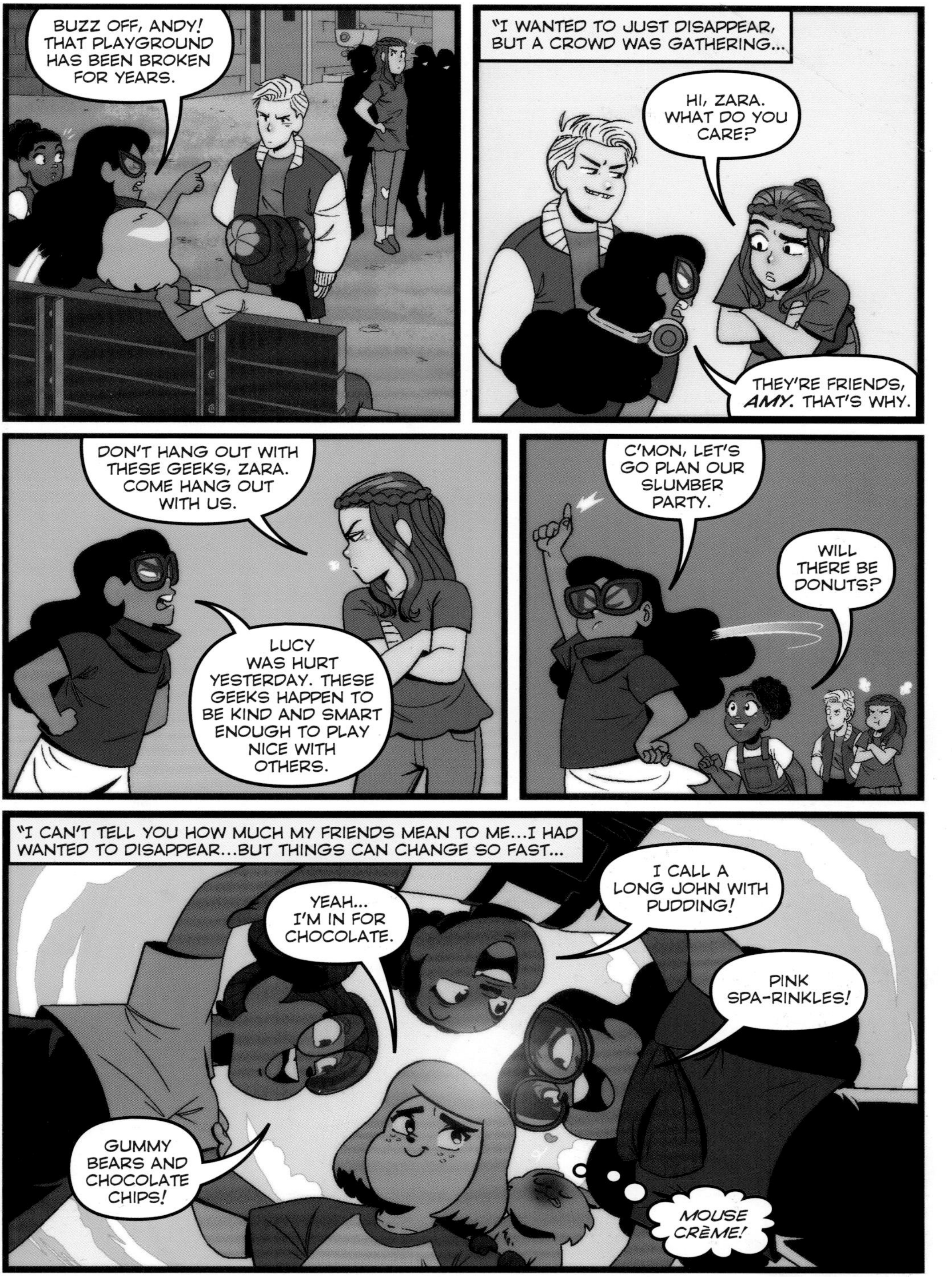
BUZZ OFF, ANDY! THAT PLAYGROUND HAS BEEN BROKEN FOR YEARS.
"I WANTED TO JUST DISAPPEAR, BUT A CROWD WAS GATHERING...
HI, ZARA. WHAT DO YOU CARE?
THEY'RE FRIENDS, *AMY*. THAT'S WHY.
DON'T HANG OUT WITH THESE GEEKS, ZARA. COME HANG OUT WITH US.
LUCY WAS HURT YESTERDAY. THESE GEEKS HAPPEN TO BE KIND AND SMART ENOUGH TO PLAY NICE WITH OTHERS.
C'MON, LET'S GO PLAN OUR SLUMBER PARTY.
WILL THERE BE DONUTS?
"I CAN'T TELL YOU HOW MUCH MY FRIENDS MEAN TO ME...I HAD WANTED TO DISAPPEAR...BUT THINGS CAN CHANGE SO FAST...
YEAH... I'M IN FOR CHOCOLATE.
I CALL A LONG JOHN WITH PUDDING!
PINK SPA-RINKLES!
GUMMY BEARS AND CHOCOLATE CHIPS!
MOUSE CRÈME!

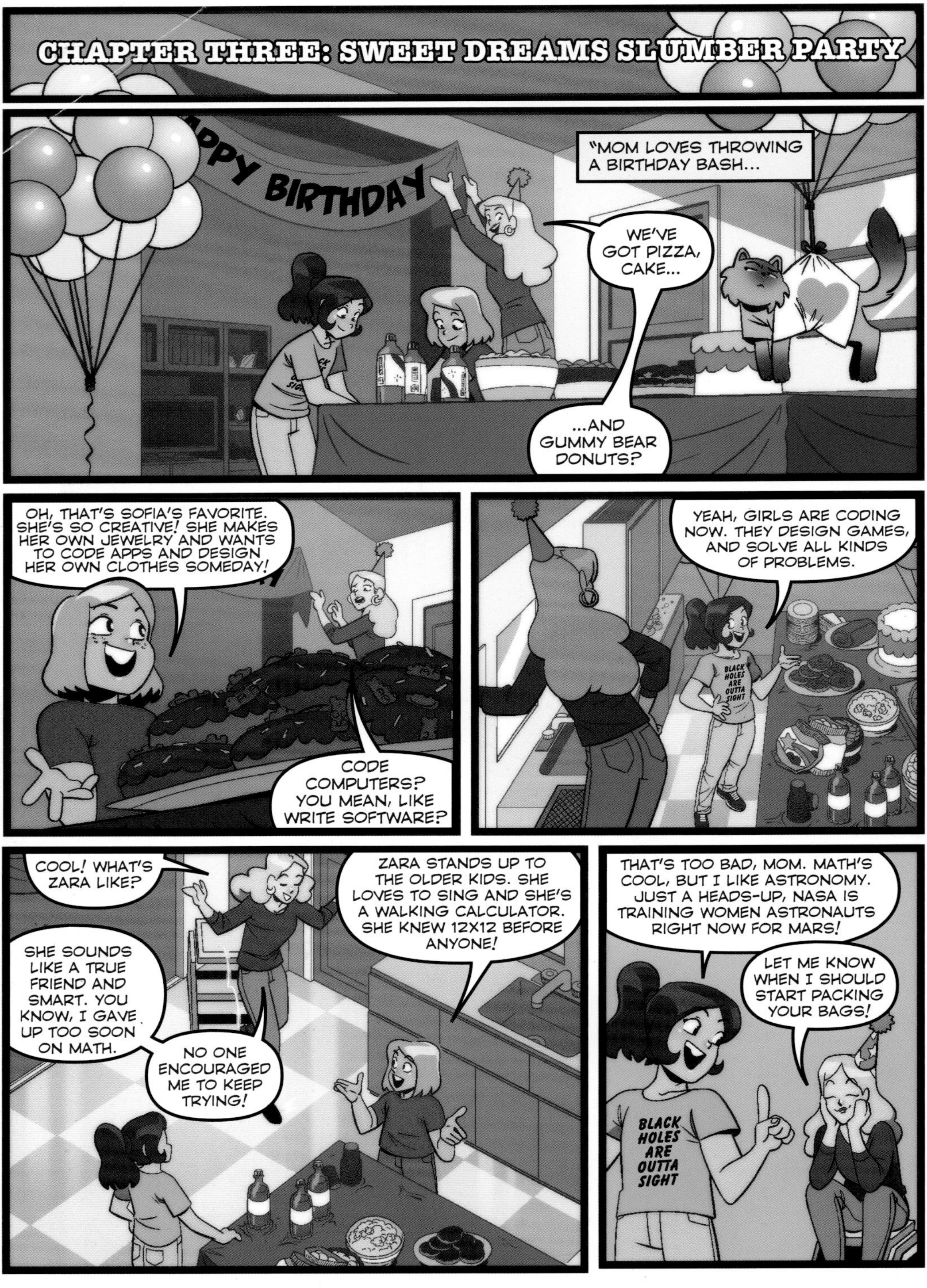
CHAPTER THREE: SWEET DREAMS SLUMBER PARTY
PPY BIRTHDAY
"MOM LOVES THROWING A BIRTHDAY BASH...
WE'VE GOT PIZZA, CAKE...
...AND GUMMY BEAR DONUTS?
OH, THAT'S SOFIA'S FAVORITE. SHE'S SO CREATIVE! SHE MAKES HER OWN JEWELRY AND WANTS TO CODE APPS AND DESIGN HER OWN CLOTHES SOMEDAY!
CODE COMPUTERS? YOU MEAN, LIKE WRITE SOFTWARE?
YEAH, GIRLS ARE CODING NOW. THEY DESIGN GAMES, AND SOLVE ALL KINDS OF PROBLEMS.
BLACK HOLES ARE OUTTA SIGHT
COOL! WHAT'S ZARA LIKE?
ZARA STANDS UP TO THE OLDER KIDS. SHE LOVES TO SING AND SHE'S A WALKING CALCULATOR. SHE KNEW 12X12 BEFORE ANYONE!
SHE SOUNDS LIKE A TRUE FRIEND AND SMART. YOU KNOW, I GAVE UP TOO SOON ON MATH.
NO ONE ENCOURAGED ME TO KEEP TRYING!
THAT'S TOO BAD, MOM. MATH'S COOL, BUT I LIKE ASTRONOMY. JUST A HEADS-UP, NASA IS TRAINING WOMEN ASTRONAUTS RIGHT NOW FOR MARS!
LET ME KNOW WHEN I SHOULD START PACKING YOUR BAGS!
BLACK HOLES ARE OUTTA SIGHT

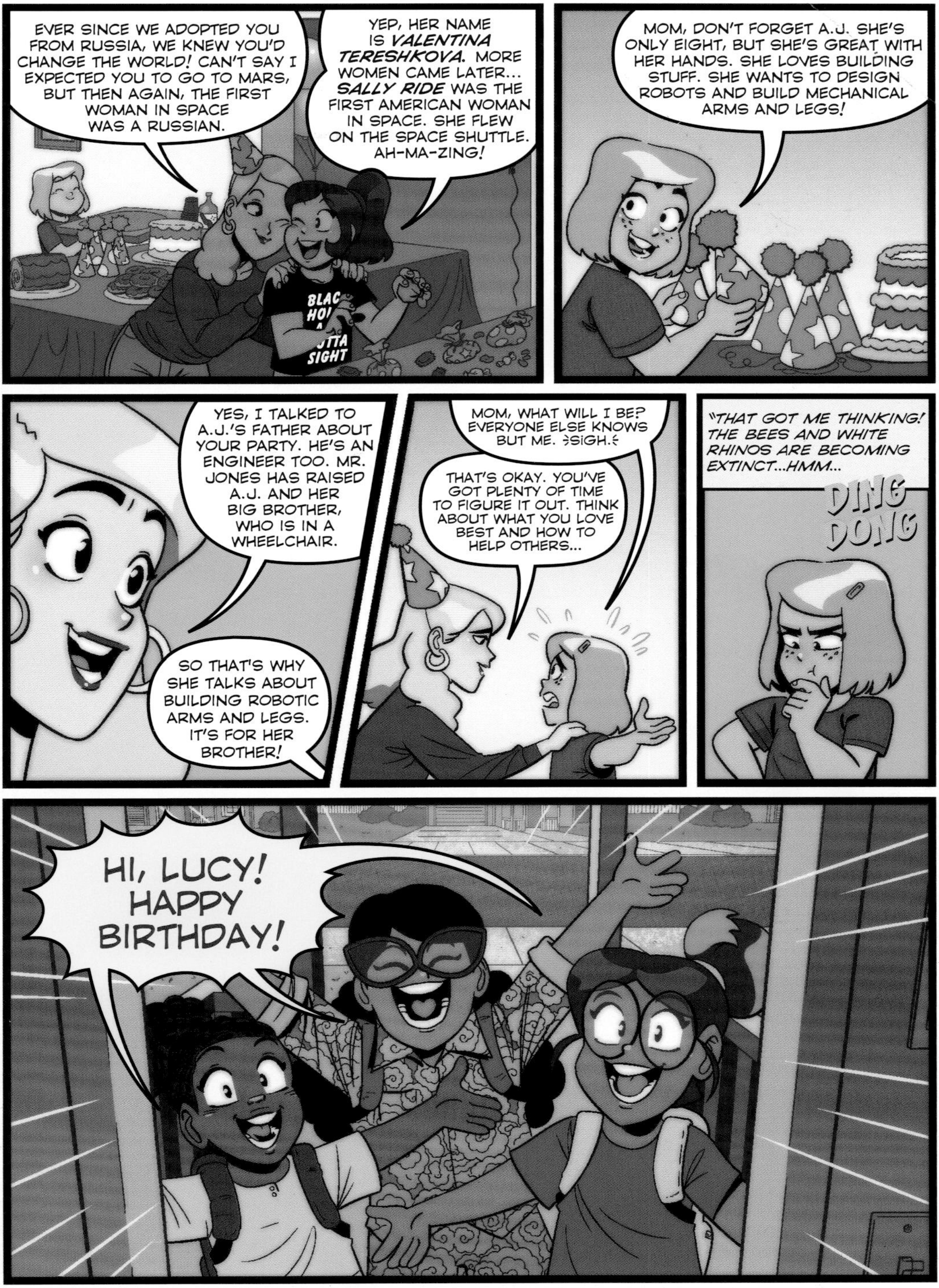
EVER SINCE WE ADOPTED YOU FROM RUSSIA, WE KNEW YOU'D CHANGE THE WORLD! CAN'T SAY I EXPECTED YOU TO GO TO MARS, BUT THEN AGAIN, THE FIRST WOMAN IN SPACE WAS A RUSSIAN.
YEP, HER NAME IS VALENTINA TERESHKOVA. MORE WOMEN CAME LATER... SALLY RIDE WAS THE FIRST AMERICAN WOMAN IN SPACE. SHE FLEW ON THE SPACE SHUTTLE. AH-MA-ZING!
MOM, DON'T FORGET A.J. SHE'S ONLY EIGHT, BUT SHE'S GREAT WITH HER HANDS. SHE LOVES BUILDING STUFF. SHE WANTS TO DESIGN ROBOTS AND BUILD MECHANICAL ARMS AND LEGS!
YES, I TALKED TO A.J.'S FATHER ABOUT YOUR PARTY. HE'S AN ENGINEER TOO. MR. JONES HAS RAISED A.J. AND HER BIG BROTHER, WHO IS IN A WHEELCHAIR.
SO THAT'S WHY SHE TALKS ABOUT BUILDING ROBOTIC ARMS AND LEGS. IT'S FOR HER BROTHER!
MOM, WHAT WILL I BE? EVERYONE ELSE KNOWS BUT ME. ≥SIGH.≤
THAT'S OKAY. YOU'VE GOT PLENTY OF TIME TO FIGURE IT OUT. THINK ABOUT WHAT YOU LOVE BEST AND HOW TO HELP OTHERS...
"THAT GOT ME THINKING! THE BEES AND WHITE RHINOS ARE BECOMING EXTINCT...HMM...
DING DONG
HI, LUCY! HAPPY BIRTHDAY!

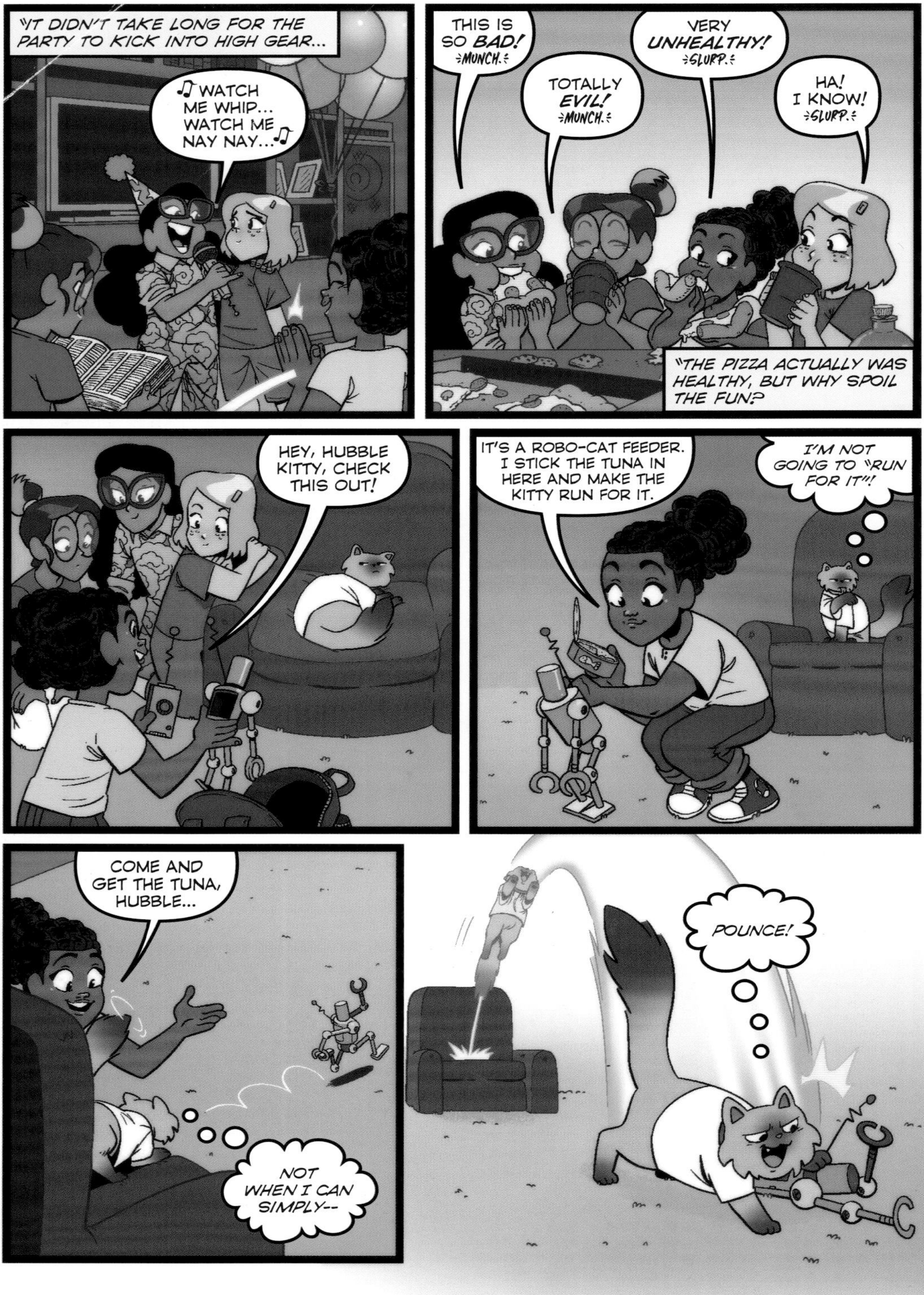
"IT DIDN'T TAKE LONG FOR THE PARTY TO KICK INTO HIGH GEAR...
♫ WATCH ME WHIP... WATCH ME NAY NAY... ♫
THIS IS SO BAD! MUNCH.
TOTALLY EVIL! MUNCH.
VERY UNHEALTHY! SLURP.
HA! I KNOW! SLURP.
"THE PIZZA ACTUALLY WAS HEALTHY, BUT WHY SPOIL THE FUN?
HEY, HUBBLE KITTY, CHECK THIS OUT!
IT'S A ROBO-CAT FEEDER. I STICK THE TUNA IN HERE AND MAKE THE KITTY RUN FOR IT.
I'M NOT GOING TO "RUN FOR IT"!
COME AND GET THE TUNA, HUBBLE...
NOT WHEN I CAN SIMPLY--
POUNCE!

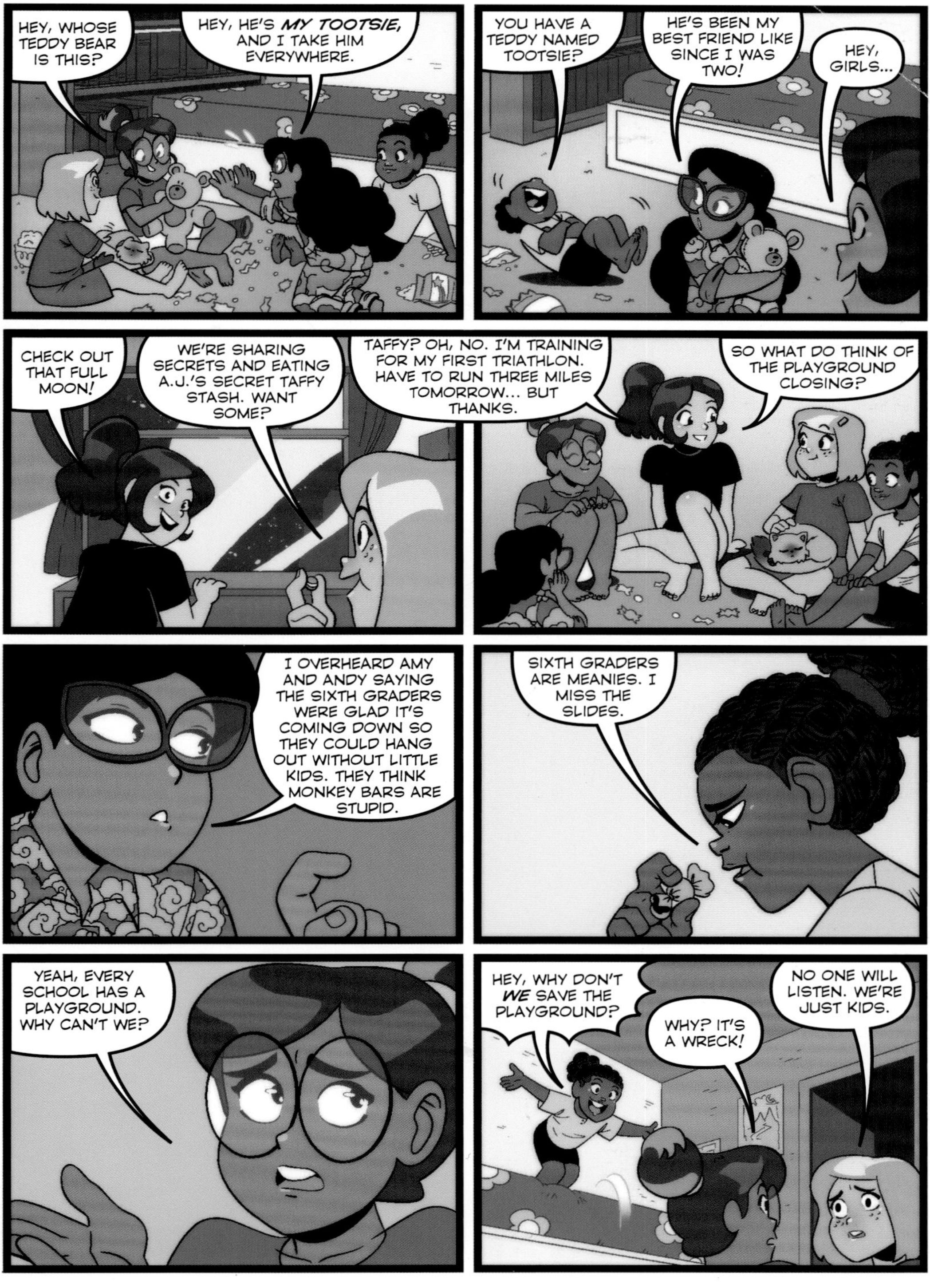
HEY, WHOSE TEDDY BEAR IS THIS?
HEY, HE'S *MY TOOTSIE,* AND I TAKE HIM EVERYWHERE.
YOU HAVE A TEDDY NAMED TOOTSIE?
HE'S BEEN MY BEST FRIEND LIKE SINCE I WAS TWO!
HEY, GIRLS...
CHECK OUT THAT FULL MOON!
WE'RE SHARING SECRETS AND EATING A.J.'S SECRET TAFFY STASH. WANT SOME?
TAFFY? OH, NO. I'M TRAINING FOR MY FIRST TRIATHLON. HAVE TO RUN THREE MILES TOMORROW... BUT THANKS.
SO WHAT DO THINK OF THE PLAYGROUND CLOSING?
I OVERHEARD AMY AND ANDY SAYING THE SIXTH GRADERS WERE GLAD IT'S COMING DOWN SO THEY COULD HANG OUT WITHOUT LITTLE KIDS. THEY THINK MONKEY BARS ARE STUPID.
SIXTH GRADERS ARE MEANIES. I MISS THE SLIDES.
YEAH, EVERY SCHOOL HAS A PLAYGROUND. WHY CAN'T WE?
HEY, WHY DON'T *WE* SAVE THE PLAYGROUND?
WHY? IT'S A WRECK!
NO ONE WILL LISTEN. WE'RE JUST KIDS.

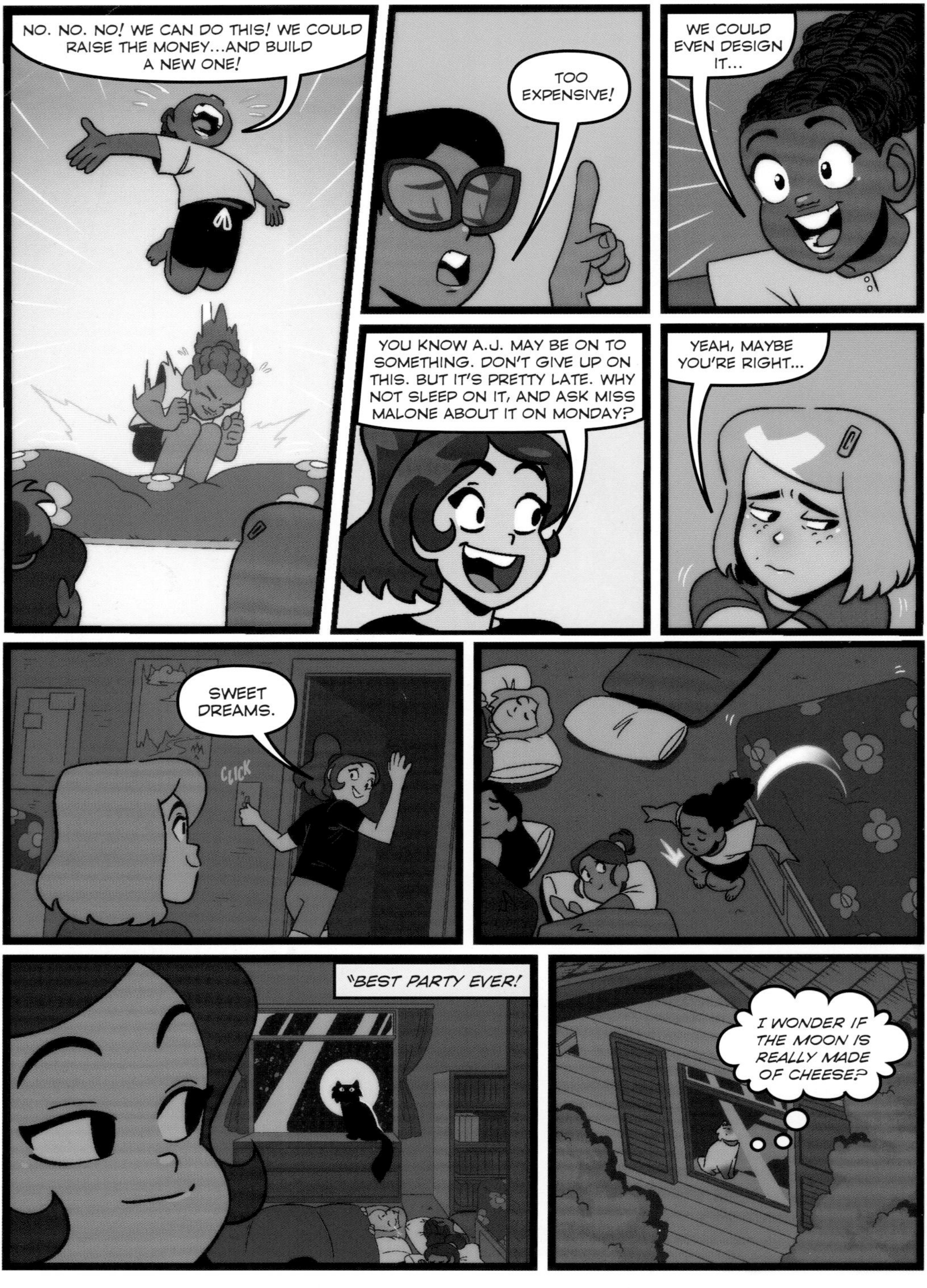
NO. NO. NO! WE CAN DO THIS! WE COULD RAISE THE MONEY...AND BUILD A NEW ONE!
TOO EXPENSIVE!
WE COULD EVEN DESIGN IT...
YOU KNOW A.J. MAY BE ON TO SOMETHING. DON'T GIVE UP ON THIS. BUT IT'S PRETTY LATE. WHY NOT SLEEP ON IT, AND ASK MISS MALONE ABOUT IT ON MONDAY?
YEAH, MAYBE YOU'RE RIGHT...
SWEET DREAMS.
CLICK
"BEST PARTY EVER!
I WONDER IF THE MOON IS REALLY MADE OF CHEESE?

CHAPTER FOUR: A BATTLE PLAN FOR ACTION

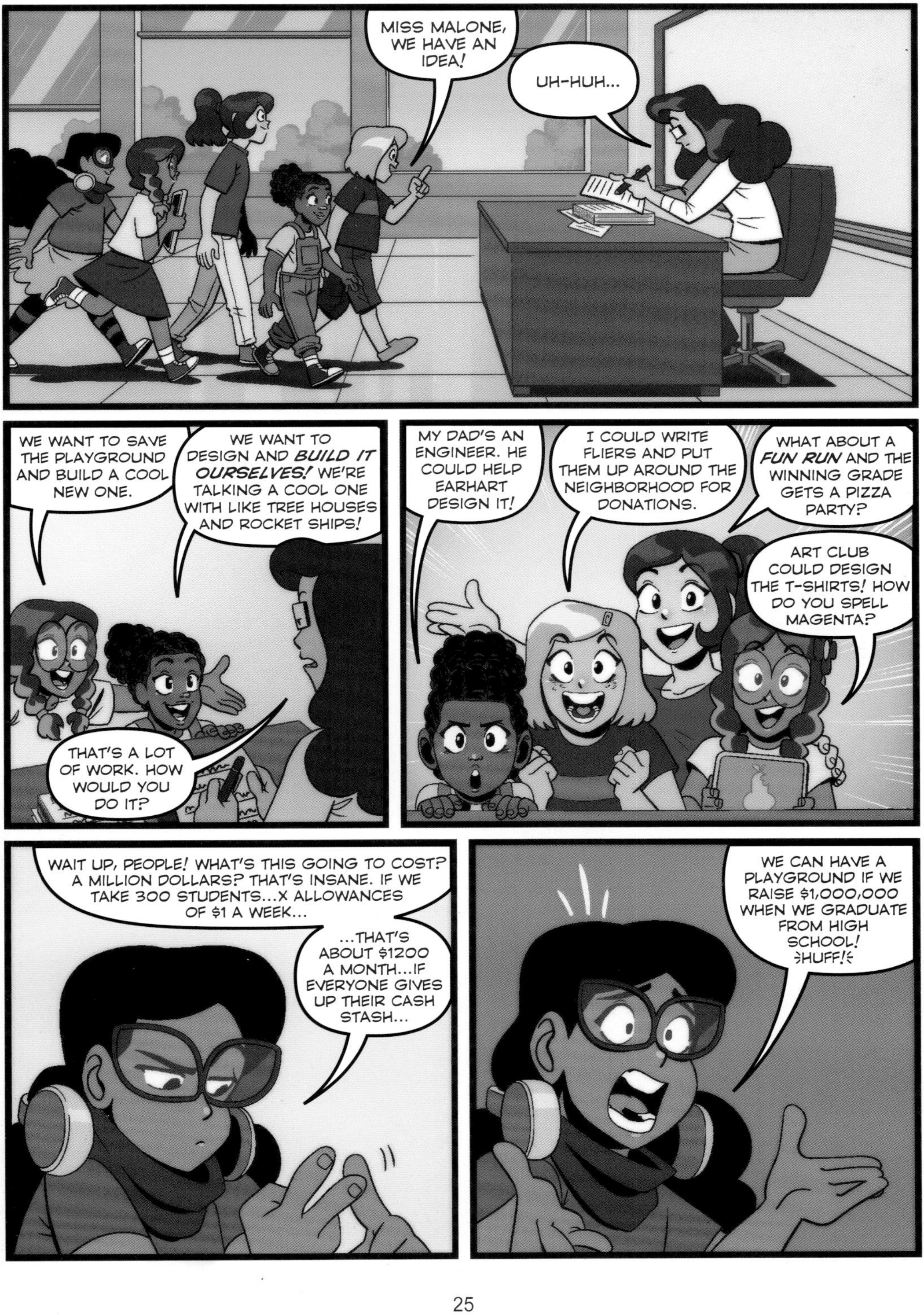

MISS MALONE, WE HAVE AN IDEA!
UH-HUH...
WE WANT TO SAVE THE PLAYGROUND AND BUILD A COOL NEW ONE.
WE WANT TO DESIGN AND BUILD IT OURSELVES! WE'RE TALKING A COOL ONE WITH LIKE TREE HOUSES AND ROCKET SHIPS!
THAT'S A LOT OF WORK. HOW WOULD YOU DO IT?
MY DAD'S AN ENGINEER. HE COULD HELP EARHART DESIGN IT!
I COULD WRITE FLIERS AND PUT THEM UP AROUND THE NEIGHBORHOOD FOR DONATIONS.
WHAT ABOUT A FUN RUN AND THE WINNING GRADE GETS A PIZZA PARTY?
ART CLUB COULD DESIGN THE T-SHIRTS! HOW DO YOU SPELL MAGENTA?
WAIT UP, PEOPLE! WHAT'S THIS GOING TO COST? A MILLION DOLLARS? THAT'S INSANE. IF WE TAKE 300 STUDENTS...X ALLOWANCES OF $1 A WEEK...
...THAT'S ABOUT $1200 A MONTH...IF EVERYONE GIVES UP THEIR CASH STASH...
WE CAN HAVE A PLAYGROUND IF WE RAISE $1,000,000 WHEN WE GRADUATE FROM HIGH SCHOOL!
HUFF!

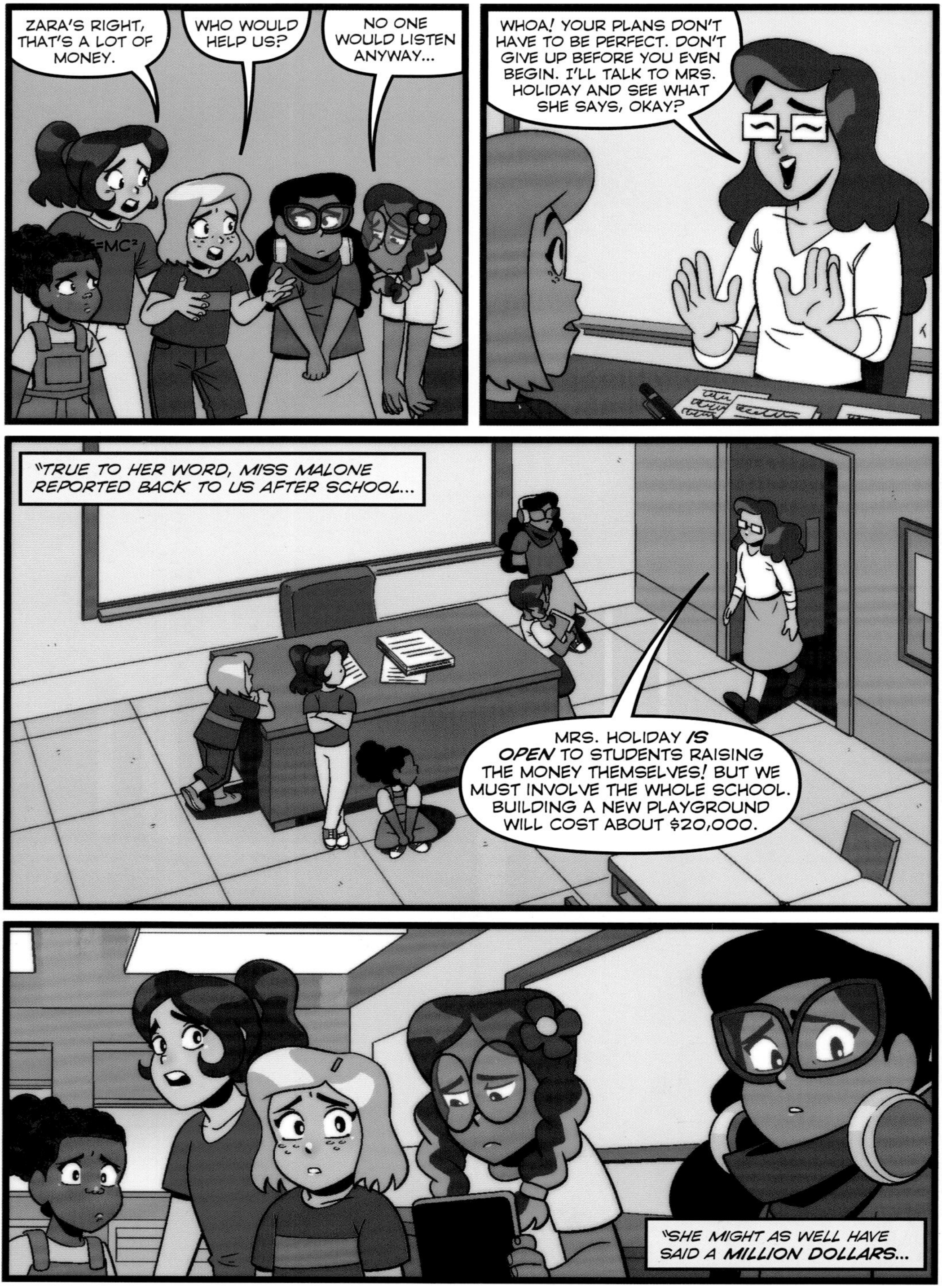
ZARA'S RIGHT, THAT'S A LOT OF MONEY.
WHO WOULD HELP US?
NO ONE WOULD LISTEN ANYWAY...
WHOA! YOUR PLANS DON'T HAVE TO BE PERFECT. DON'T GIVE UP BEFORE YOU EVEN BEGIN. I'LL TALK TO MRS. HOLIDAY AND SEE WHAT SHE SAYS, OKAY?
"TRUE TO HER WORD, MISS MALONE REPORTED BACK TO US AFTER SCHOOL...
MRS. HOLIDAY ***IS OPEN*** TO STUDENTS RAISING THE MONEY THEMSELVES! BUT WE MUST INVOLVE THE WHOLE SCHOOL. BUILDING A NEW PLAYGROUND WILL COST ABOUT $20,000.
"SHE MIGHT AS WELL HAVE SAID A ***MILLION DOLLARS***...

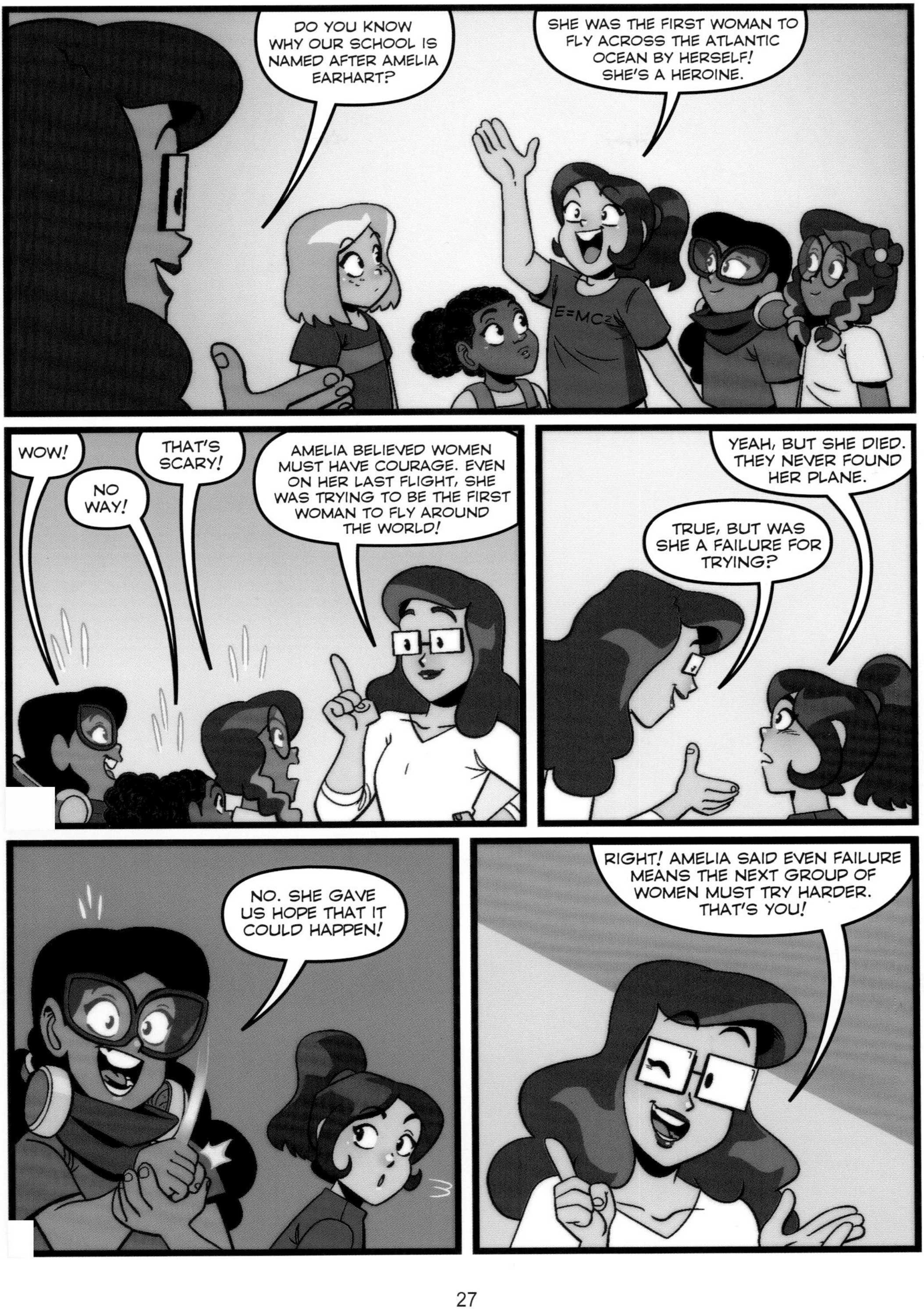
DO YOU KNOW WHY OUR SCHOOL IS NAMED AFTER AMELIA EARHART?
SHE WAS THE FIRST WOMAN TO FLY ACROSS THE ATLANTIC OCEAN BY HERSELF! SHE'S A HEROINE.
E=MC2
WOW!
NO WAY!
THAT'S SCARY!
AMELIA BELIEVED WOMEN MUST HAVE COURAGE. EVEN ON HER LAST FLIGHT, SHE WAS TRYING TO BE THE FIRST WOMAN TO FLY AROUND THE WORLD!
YEAH, BUT SHE DIED. THEY NEVER FOUND HER PLANE.
TRUE, BUT WAS SHE A FAILURE FOR TRYING?
NO. SHE GAVE US HOPE THAT IT COULD HAPPEN!
RIGHT! AMELIA SAID EVEN FAILURE MEANS THE NEXT GROUP OF WOMEN MUST TRY HARDER. THAT'S YOU!

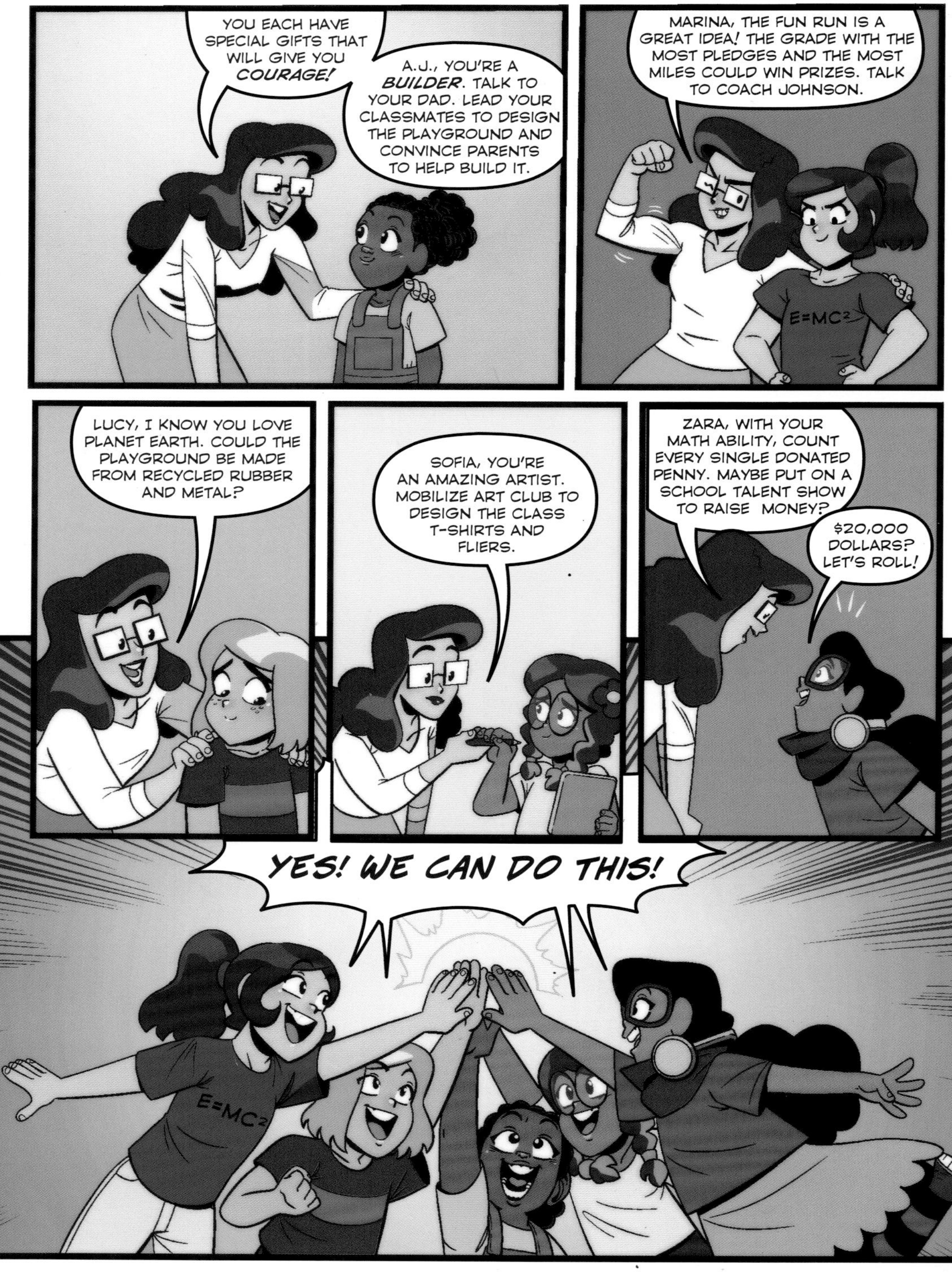
YOU EACH HAVE SPECIAL GIFTS THAT WILL GIVE YOU *COURAGE!*
A.J., YOU'RE A ***BUILDER***. TALK TO YOUR DAD. LEAD YOUR CLASSMATES TO DESIGN THE PLAYGROUND AND CONVINCE PARENTS TO HELP BUILD IT.
MARINA, THE FUN RUN IS A GREAT IDEA! THE GRADE WITH THE MOST PLEDGES AND THE MOST MILES COULD WIN PRIZES. TALK TO COACH JOHNSON.
E=MC²
LUCY, I KNOW YOU LOVE PLANET EARTH. COULD THE PLAYGROUND BE MADE FROM RECYCLED RUBBER AND METAL?
SOFIA, YOU'RE AN AMAZING ARTIST. MOBILIZE ART CLUB TO DESIGN THE CLASS T-SHIRTS AND FLIERS.
ZARA, WITH YOUR MATH ABILITY, COUNT EVERY SINGLE DONATED PENNY. MAYBE PUT ON A SCHOOL TALENT SHOW TO RAISE MONEY?
$20,000 DOLLARS? LET'S ROLL!
YES! WE CAN DO THIS!
E=MC²

CHAPTER FIVE: GET READY...SET...

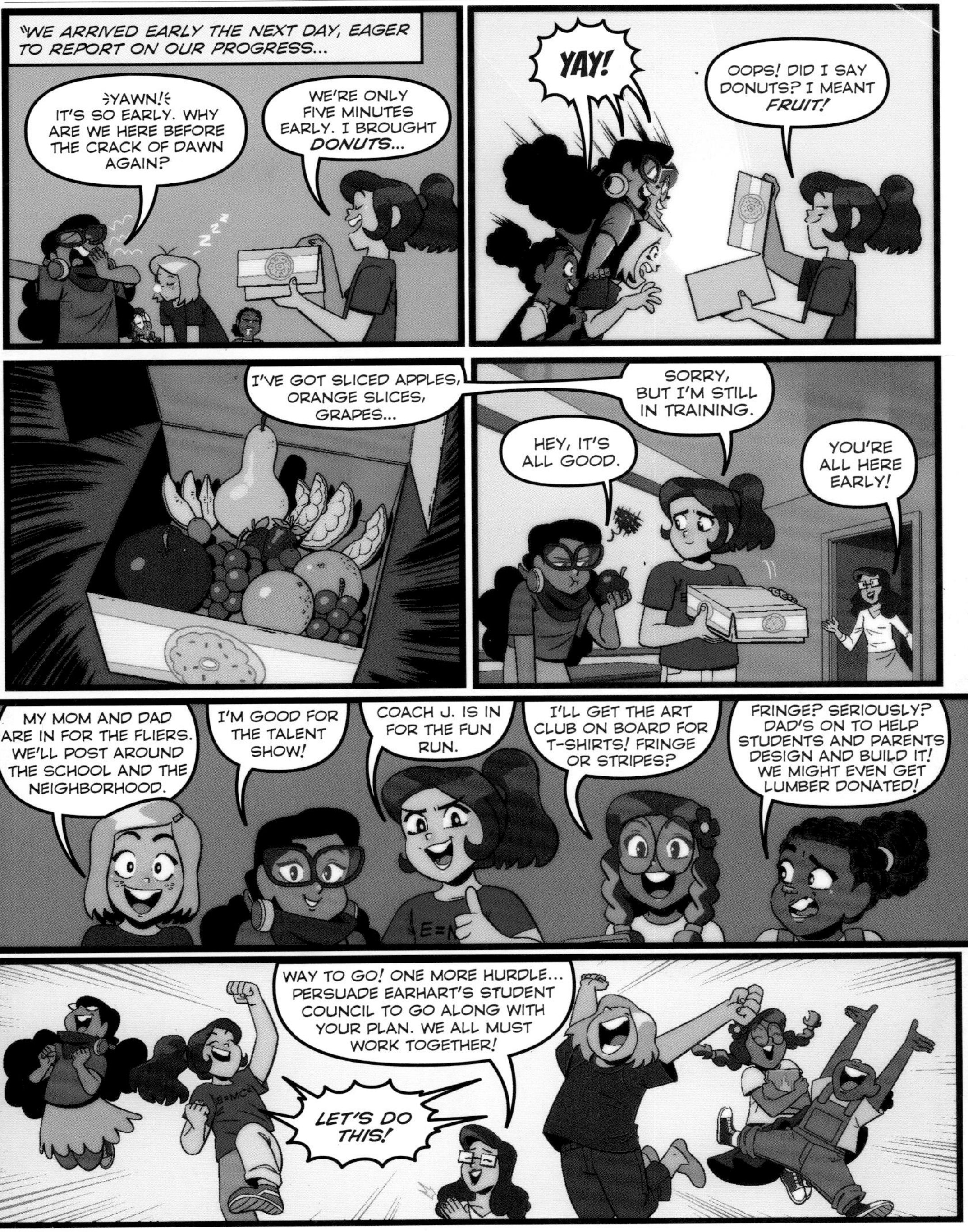

"WE ARRIVED EARLY THE NEXT DAY, EAGER TO REPORT ON OUR PROGRESS...
YAWN! IT'S SO EARLY. WHY ARE WE HERE BEFORE THE CRACK OF DAWN AGAIN?
WE'RE ONLY FIVE MINUTES EARLY. I BROUGHT DONUTS...
YAY!
OOPS! DID I SAY DONUTS? I MEANT FRUIT!
I'VE GOT SLICED APPLES, ORANGE SLICES, GRAPES...
SORRY, BUT I'M STILL IN TRAINING.
HEY, IT'S ALL GOOD.
YOU'RE ALL HERE EARLY!
MY MOM AND DAD ARE IN FOR THE FLIERS. WE'LL POST AROUND THE SCHOOL AND THE NEIGHBORHOOD.
I'M GOOD FOR THE TALENT SHOW!
COACH J. IS IN FOR THE FUN RUN.
I'LL GET THE ART CLUB ON BOARD FOR T-SHIRTS! FRINGE OR STRIPES?
FRINGE? SERIOUSLY? DAD'S ON TO HELP STUDENTS AND PARENTS DESIGN AND BUILD IT! WE MIGHT EVEN GET LUMBER DONATED!
WAY TO GO! ONE MORE HURDLE... PERSUADE EARHART'S STUDENT COUNCIL TO GO ALONG WITH YOUR PLAN. WE ALL MUST WORK TOGETHER!
LET'S DO THIS!

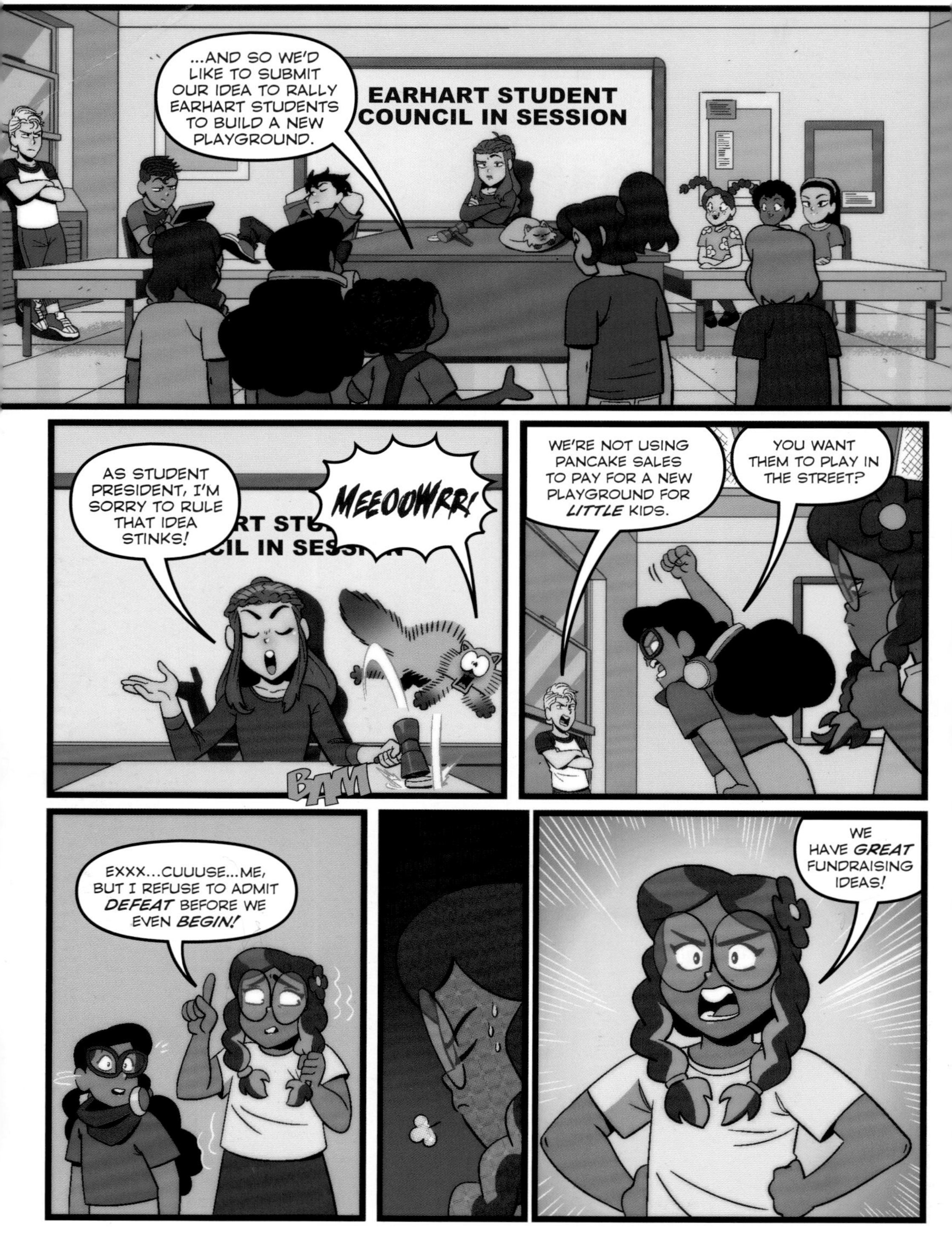
...AND SO WE'D LIKE TO SUBMIT OUR IDEA TO RALLY EARHART STUDENTS TO BUILD A NEW PLAYGROUND.
EARHART STUDENT COUNCIL IN SESSION
AS STUDENT PRESIDENT, I'M SORRY TO RULE THAT IDEA STINKS!
MEEOOWRR!
BAM
WE'RE NOT USING PANCAKE SALES TO PAY FOR A NEW PLAYGROUND FOR LITTLE KIDS.
YOU WANT THEM TO PLAY IN THE STREET?
EXXX...CUUUSE...ME, BUT I REFUSE TO ADMIT DEFEAT BEFORE WE EVEN BEGIN!
WE HAVE GREAT FUNDRAISING IDEAS!

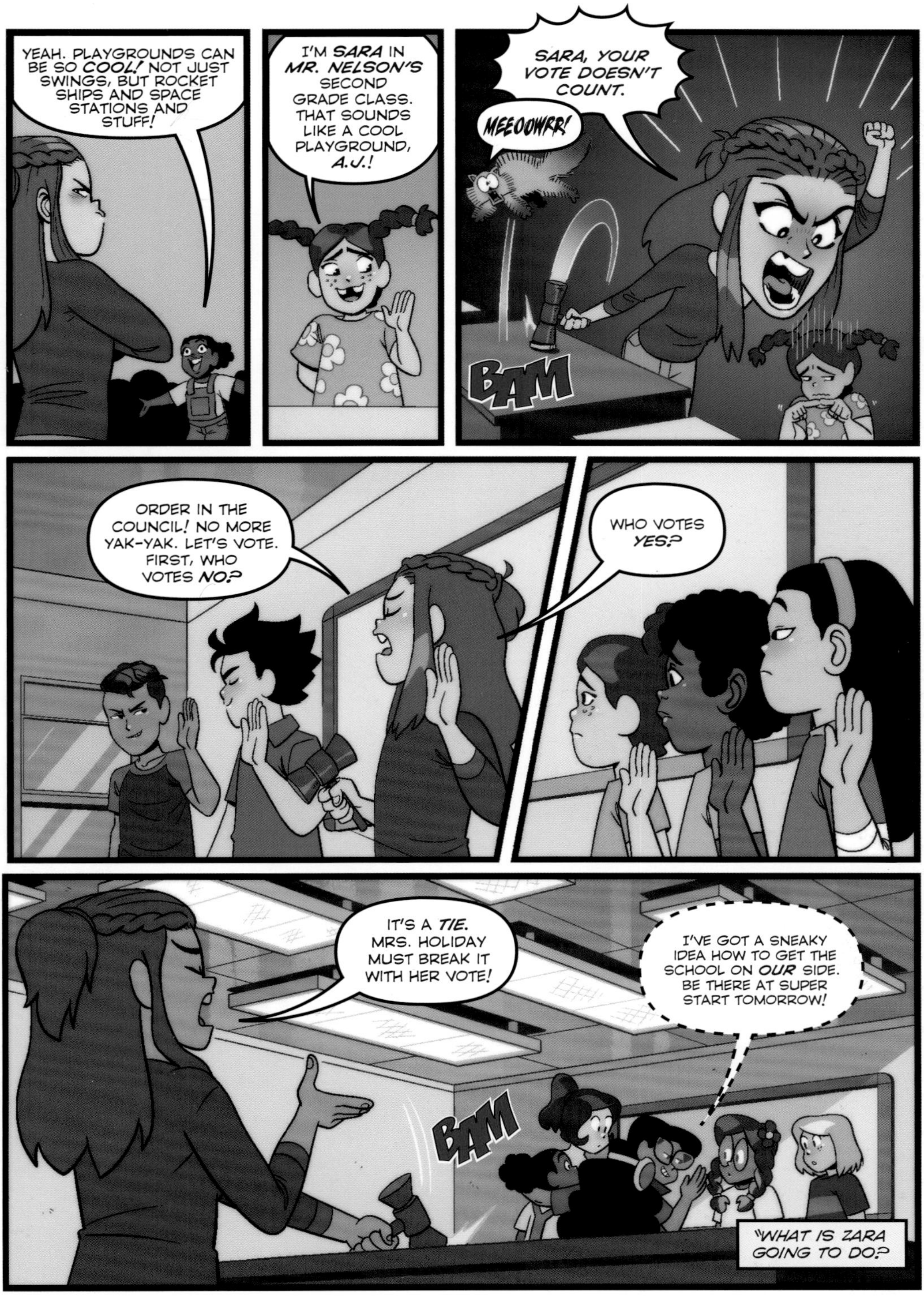
YEAH. PLAYGROUNDS CAN BE SO COOL! NOT JUST SWINGS, BUT ROCKET SHIPS AND SPACE STATIONS AND STUFF!
I'M SARA IN MR. NELSON'S SECOND GRADE CLASS. THAT SOUNDS LIKE A COOL PLAYGROUND, A.J.!
SARA, YOUR VOTE DOESN'T COUNT.
MEEOOWRR!
BAM
ORDER IN THE COUNCIL! NO MORE YAK-YAK. LET'S VOTE. FIRST, WHO VOTES NO?
WHO VOTES YES?
IT'S A TIE. MRS. HOLIDAY MUST BREAK IT WITH HER VOTE!
I'VE GOT A SNEAKY IDEA HOW TO GET THE SCHOOL ON OUR SIDE. BE THERE AT SUPER START TOMORROW!
BAM
"WHAT IS ZARA GOING TO DO?

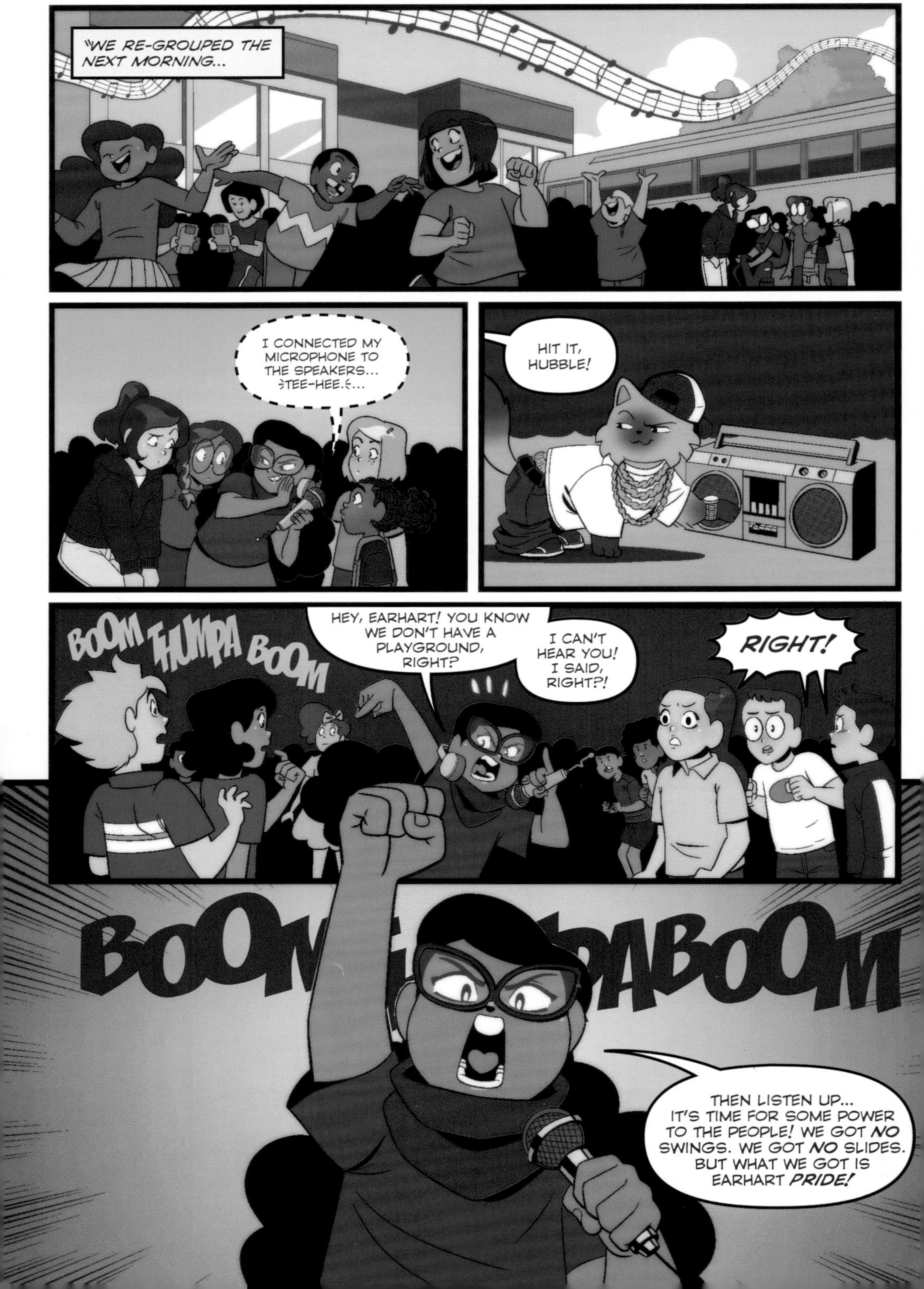
"WE RE-GROUPED THE NEXT MORNING...
I CONNECTED MY MICROPHONE TO THE SPEAKERS... TEE-HEE...
HIT IT, HUBBLE!
BOOM THUMPA BOOM
HEY, EARHART! YOU KNOW WE DON'T HAVE A PLAYGROUND, RIGHT?
I CAN'T HEAR YOU! I SAID, RIGHT?!
RIGHT!
THEN LISTEN UP... IT'S TIME FOR SOME POWER TO THE PEOPLE! WE GOT NO SWINGS. WE GOT NO SLIDES. BUT WHAT WE GOT IS EARHART PRIDE!

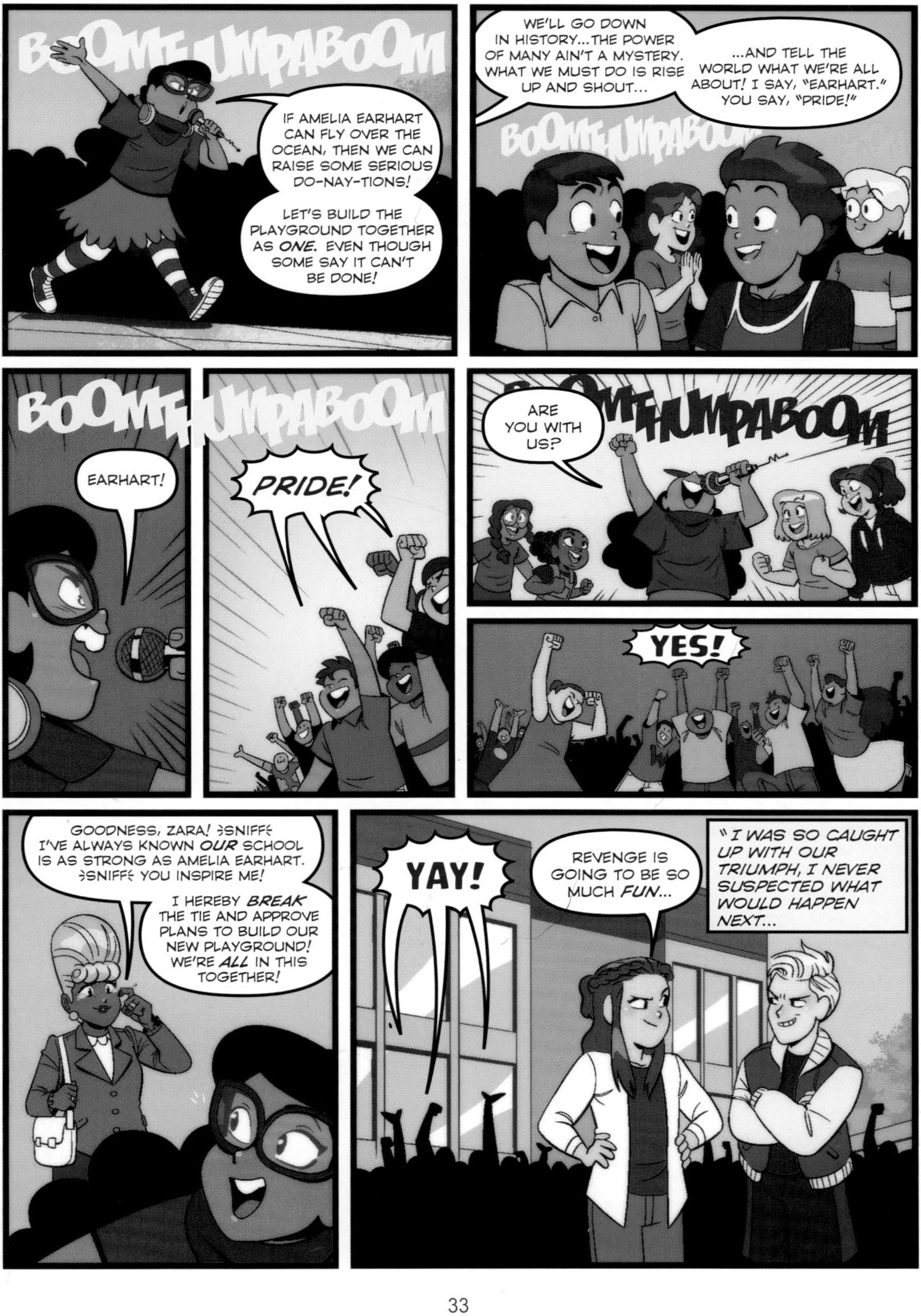
BOOMTHUMPABOOM
IF AMELIA EARHART CAN FLY OVER THE OCEAN, THEN WE CAN RAISE SOME SERIOUS DO-NAY-TIONS!
LET'S BUILD THE PLAYGROUND TOGETHER AS ONE. EVEN THOUGH SOME SAY IT CAN'T BE DONE!
WE'LL GO DOWN IN HISTORY...THE POWER OF MANY AIN'T A MYSTERY. WHAT WE MUST DO IS RISE UP AND SHOUT...
...AND TELL THE WORLD WHAT WE'RE ALL ABOUT! I SAY, "EARHART." YOU SAY, "PRIDE!"
BOOMTHUMPABOOM
EARHART!
PRIDE!
ARE YOU WITH US?
YES!
GOODNESS, ZARA! >SNIFF< I'VE ALWAYS KNOWN OUR SCHOOL IS AS STRONG AS AMELIA EARHART. >SNIFF< YOU INSPIRE ME!
I HEREBY BREAK THE TIE AND APPROVE PLANS TO BUILD OUR NEW PLAYGROUND! WE'RE ALL IN THIS TOGETHER!
YAY!
REVENGE IS GOING TO BE SO MUCH FUN...
"I WAS SO CAUGHT UP WITH OUR TRIUMPH, I NEVER SUSPECTED WHAT WOULD HAPPEN NEXT...

CHAPTER SIX : ...GO! EARHART BANDS TOGETHER.

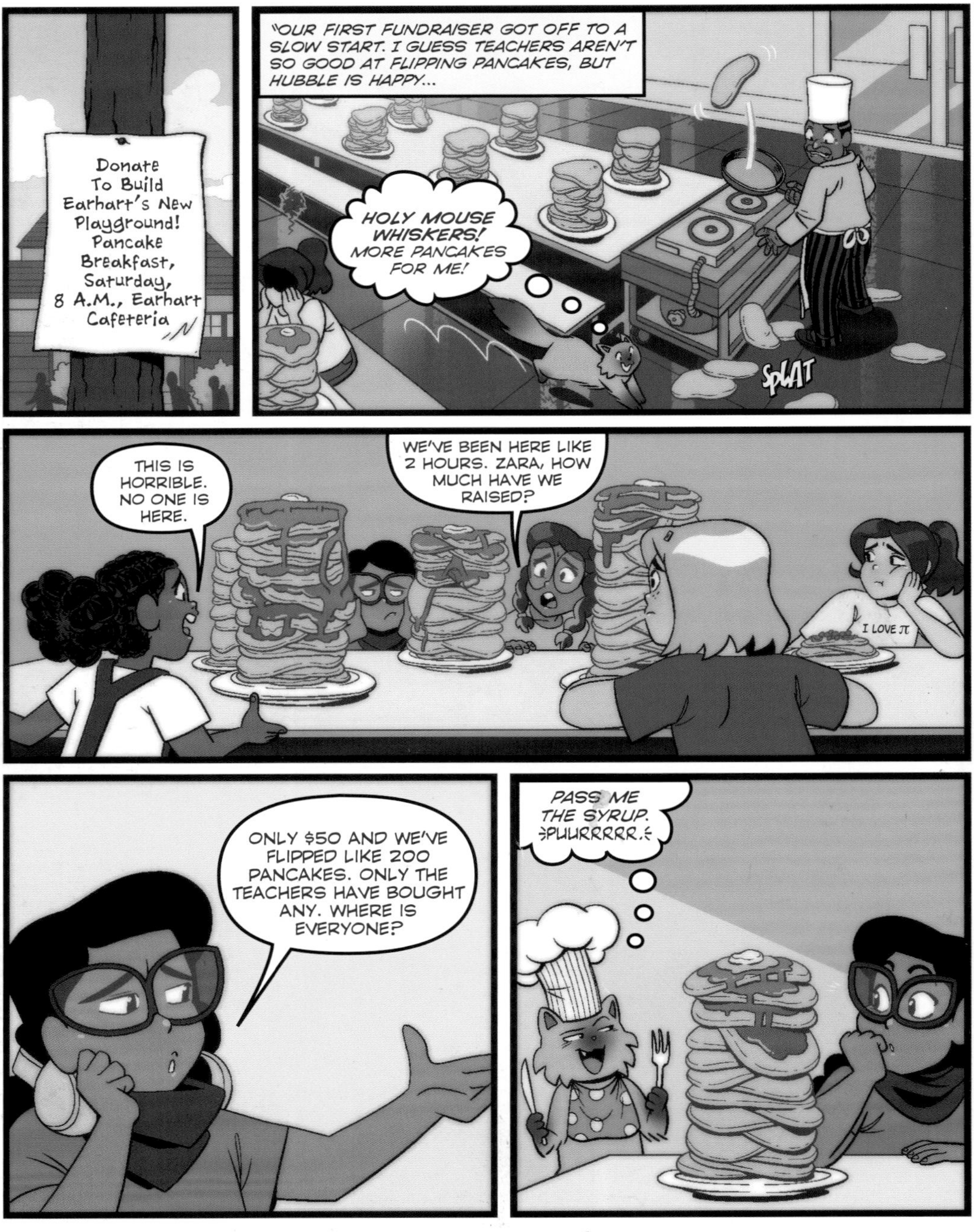

Donate To Build Earhart's New Playground! Pancake Breakfast, Saturday, 8 A.M., Earhart Cafeteria
"OUR FIRST FUNDRAISER GOT OFF TO A SLOW START. I GUESS TEACHERS AREN'T SO GOOD AT FLIPPING PANCAKES, BUT HUBBLE IS HAPPY...
HOLY MOUSE WHISKERS! MORE PANCAKES FOR ME!
SPLAT
THIS IS HORRIBLE. NO ONE IS HERE.
WE'VE BEEN HERE LIKE 2 HOURS. ZARA, HOW MUCH HAVE WE RAISED?
I LOVE π
ONLY $50 AND WE'VE FLIPPED LIKE 200 PANCAKES. ONLY THE TEACHERS HAVE BOUGHT ANY. WHERE IS EVERYONE?
PASS ME THE SYRUP. PUURRRRR.

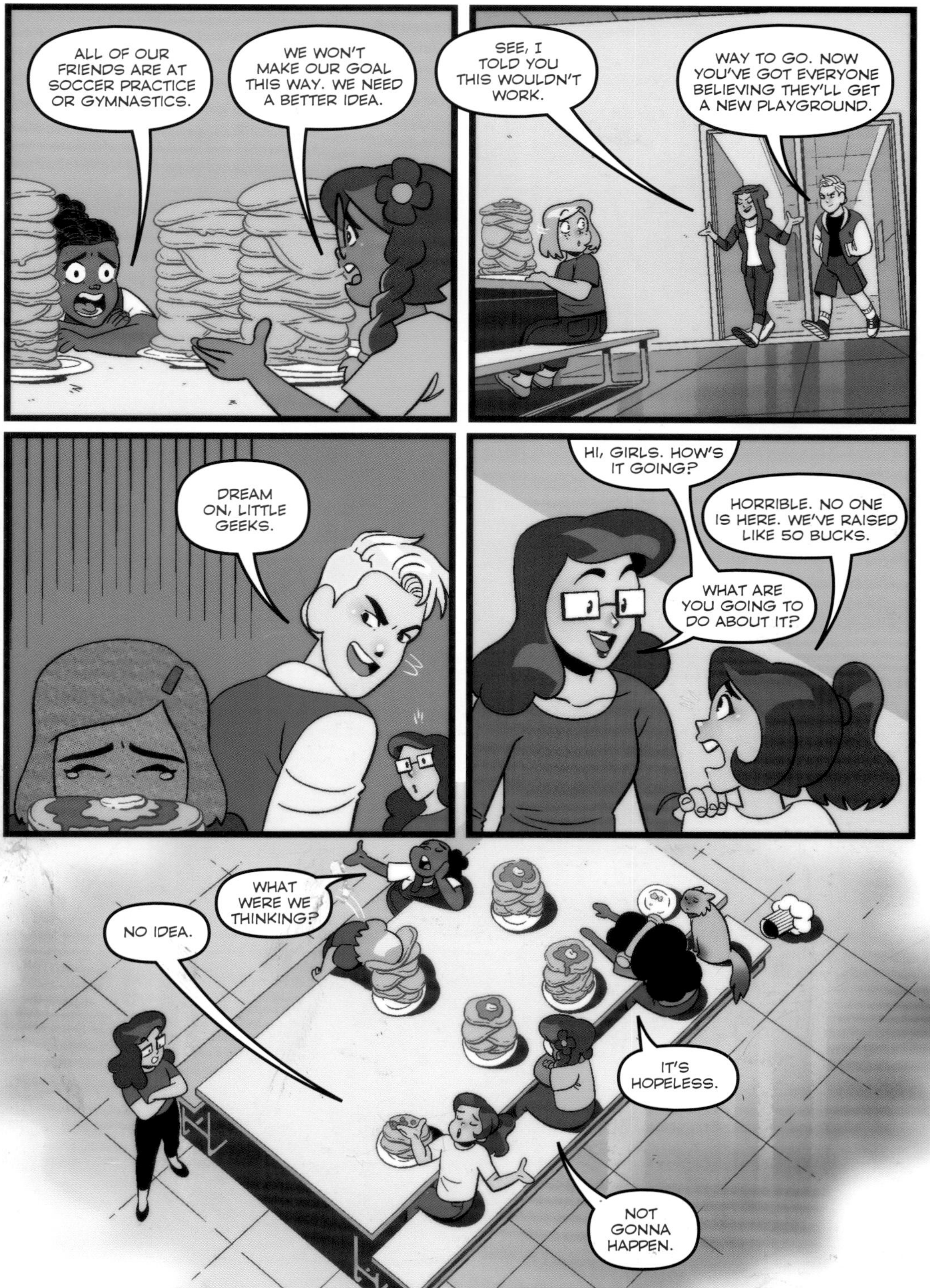
ALL OF OUR FRIENDS ARE AT SOCCER PRACTICE OR GYMNASTICS.
WE WON'T MAKE OUR GOAL THIS WAY. WE NEED A BETTER IDEA.
SEE, I TOLD YOU THIS WOULDN'T WORK.
WAY TO GO. NOW YOU'VE GOT EVERYONE BELIEVING THEY'LL GET A NEW PLAYGROUND.
DREAM ON, LITTLE GEEKS.
HI, GIRLS. HOW'S IT GOING?
HORRIBLE. NO ONE IS HERE. WE'VE RAISED LIKE 50 BUCKS.
WHAT ARE YOU GOING TO DO ABOUT IT?
WHAT WERE WE THINKING?
NO IDEA.
IT'S HOPELESS.
NOT GONNA HAPPEN.

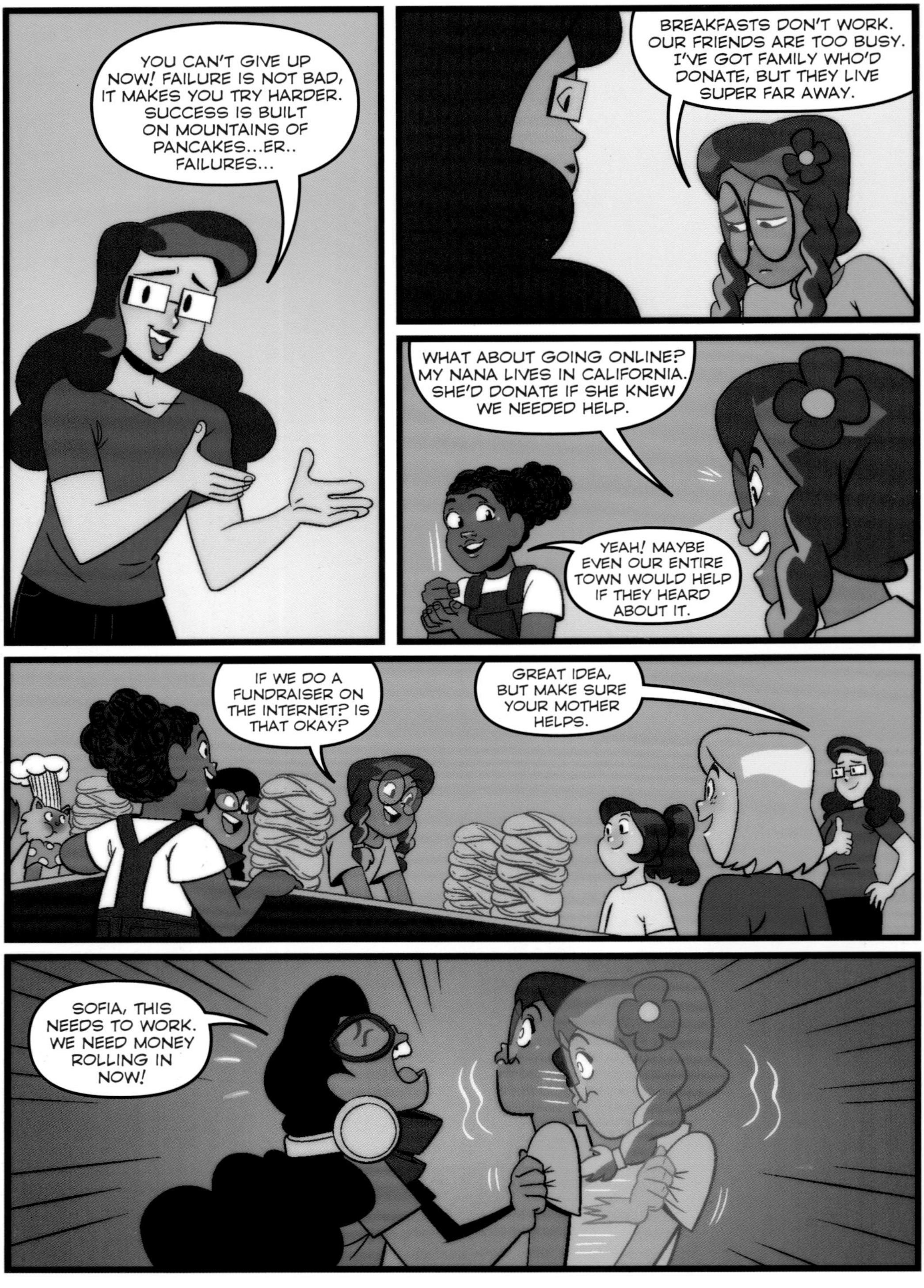
YOU CAN'T GIVE UP NOW! FAILURE IS NOT BAD, IT MAKES YOU TRY HARDER. SUCCESS IS BUILT ON MOUNTAINS OF PANCAKES...ER.. FAILURES...
BREAKFASTS DON'T WORK. OUR FRIENDS ARE TOO BUSY. I'VE GOT FAMILY WHO'D DONATE, BUT THEY LIVE SUPER FAR AWAY.
WHAT ABOUT GOING ONLINE? MY NANA LIVES IN CALIFORNIA. SHE'D DONATE IF SHE KNEW WE NEEDED HELP.
YEAH! MAYBE EVEN OUR ENTIRE TOWN WOULD HELP IF THEY HEARD ABOUT IT.
IF WE DO A FUNDRAISER ON THE INTERNET? IS THAT OKAY?
GREAT IDEA, BUT MAKE SURE YOUR MOTHER HELPS.
SOFIA, THIS NEEDS TO WORK. WE NEED MONEY ROLLING IN NOW!

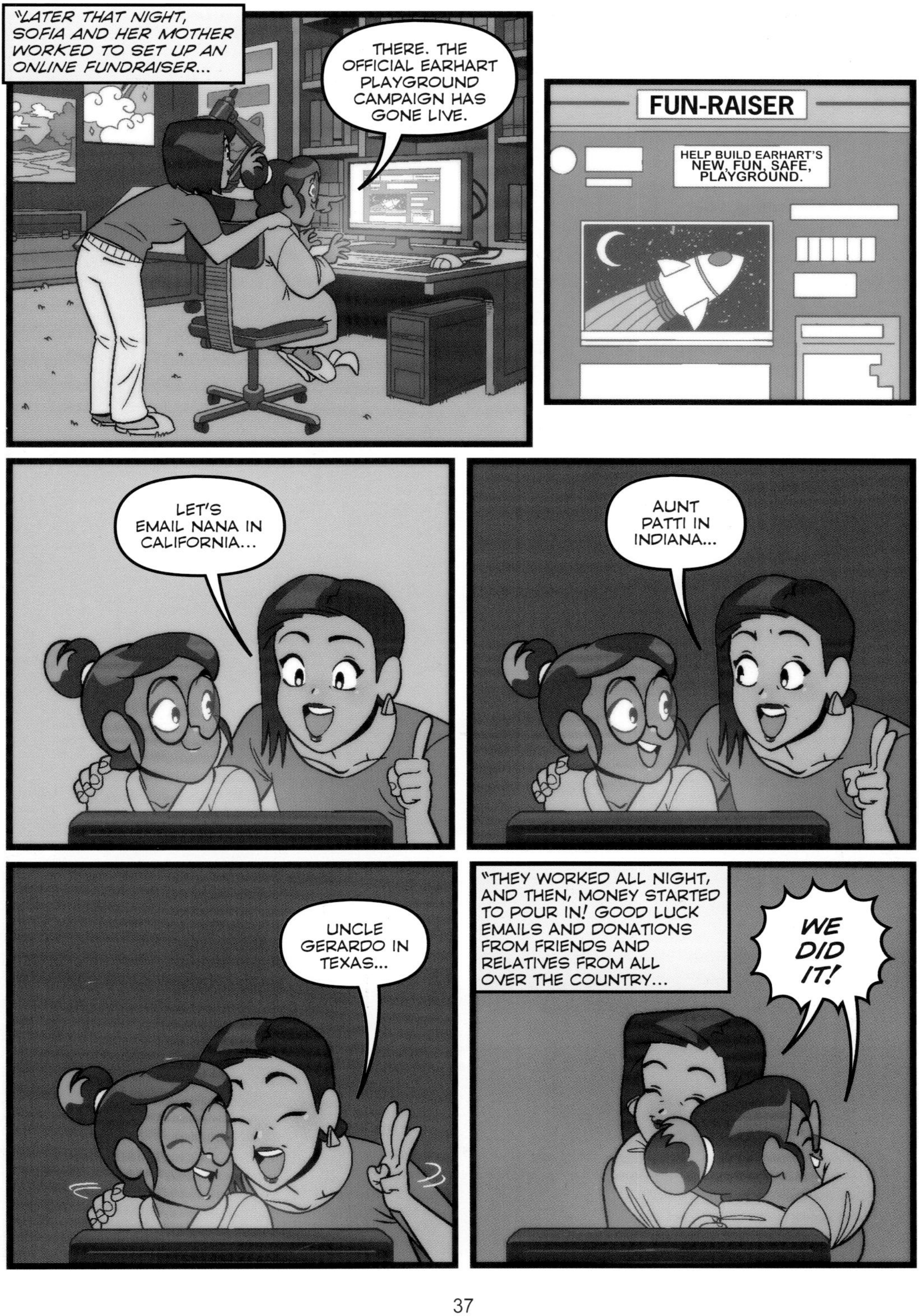
"LATER THAT NIGHT, SOFIA AND HER MOTHER WORKED TO SET UP AN ONLINE FUNDRAISER...
THERE. THE OFFICIAL EARHART PLAYGROUND CAMPAIGN HAS GONE LIVE.
FUN-RAISER
HELP BUILD EARHART'S NEW, FUN, SAFE, PLAYGROUND.
LET'S EMAIL NANA IN CALIFORNIA...
AUNT PATTI IN INDIANA...
UNCLE GERARDO IN TEXAS...
"THEY WORKED ALL NIGHT, AND THEN, MONEY STARTED TO POUR IN! GOOD LUCK EMAILS AND DONATIONS FROM FRIENDS AND RELATIVES FROM ALL OVER THE COUNTRY...
WE DID IT!

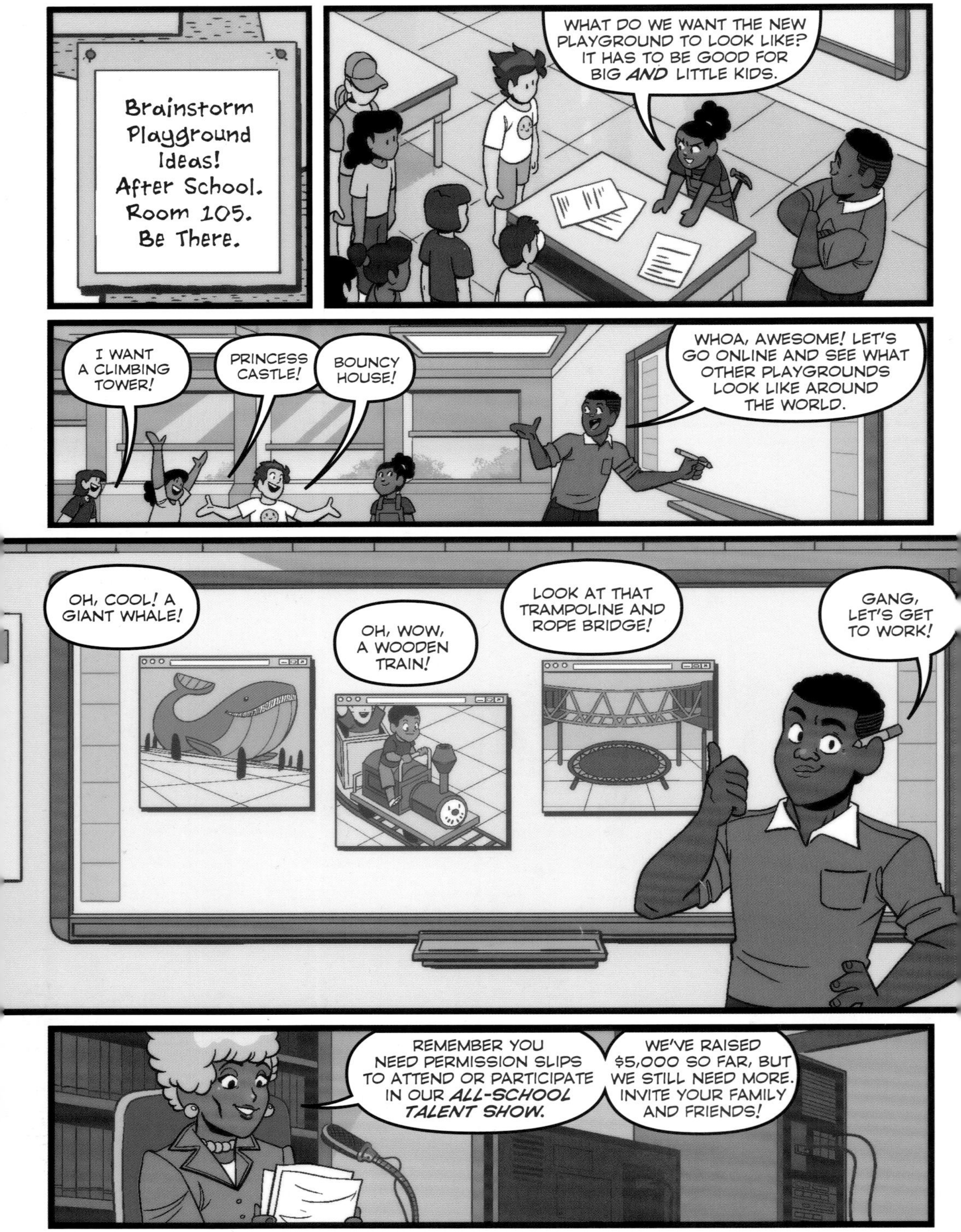
Brainstorm Playground Ideas! After School. Room 105. Be There.
WHAT DO WE WANT THE NEW PLAYGROUND TO LOOK LIKE? IT HAS TO BE GOOD FOR BIG AND LITTLE KIDS.
I WANT A CLIMBING TOWER!
PRINCESS CASTLE!
BOUNCY HOUSE!
WHOA, AWESOME! LET'S GO ONLINE AND SEE WHAT OTHER PLAYGROUNDS LOOK LIKE AROUND THE WORLD.
OH, COOL! A GIANT WHALE!
OH, WOW, A WOODEN TRAIN!
LOOK AT THAT TRAMPOLINE AND ROPE BRIDGE!
GANG, LET'S GET TO WORK!
REMEMBER YOU NEED PERMISSION SLIPS TO ATTEND OR PARTICIPATE IN OUR ALL-SCHOOL TALENT SHOW.
WE'VE RAISED $5,000 SO FAR, BUT WE STILL NEED MORE. INVITE YOUR FAMILY AND FRIENDS!

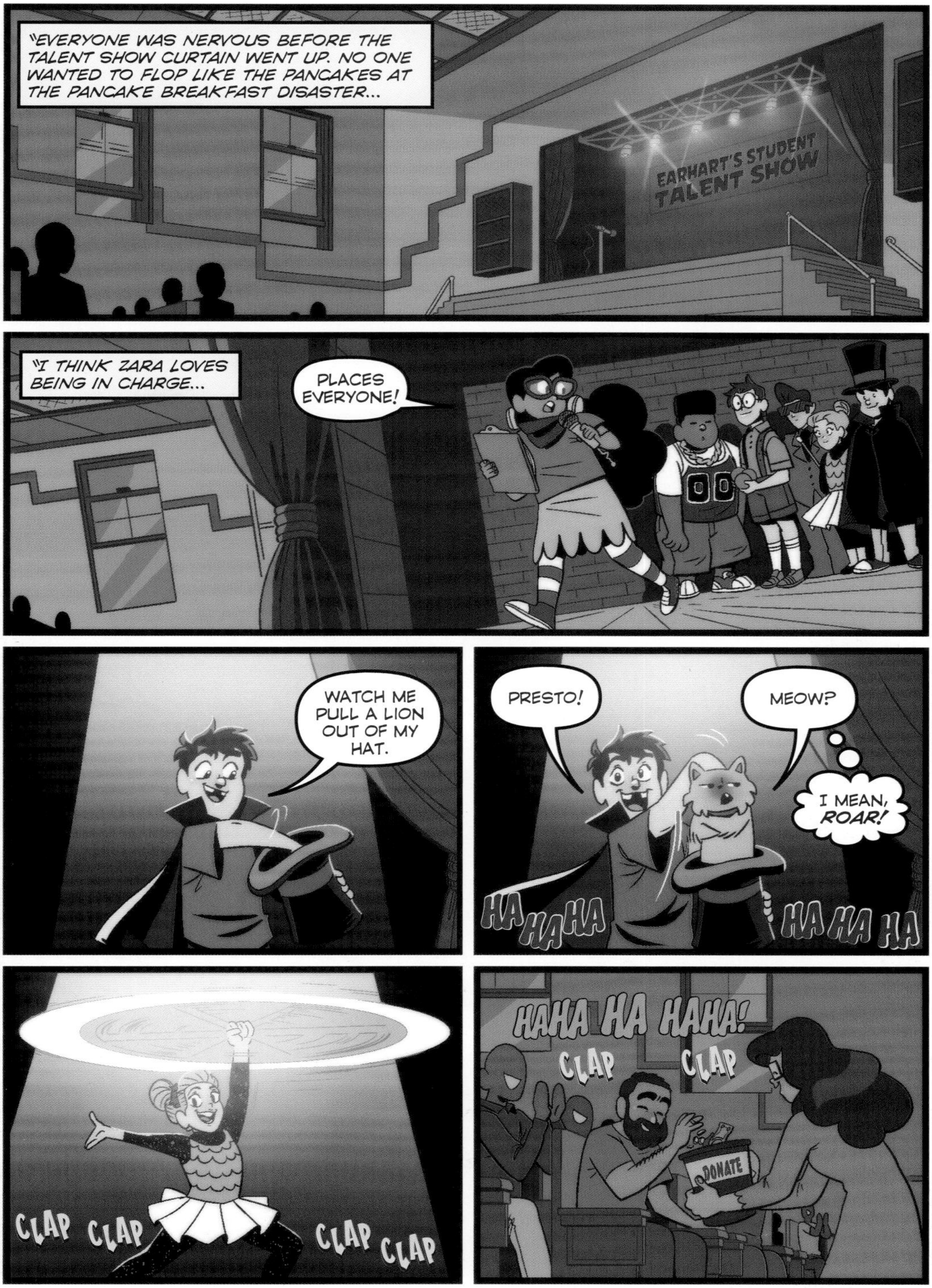
"EVERYONE WAS NERVOUS BEFORE THE TALENT SHOW CURTAIN WENT UP. NO ONE WANTED TO FLOP LIKE THE PANCAKES AT THE PANCAKE BREAKFAST DISASTER...
EARHART'S STUDENT TALENT SHOW
"I THINK ZARA LOVES BEING IN CHARGE...
PLACES EVERYONE!
WATCH ME PULL A LION OUT OF MY HAT.
PRESTO!
MEOW?
I MEAN, ROAR!
HA HA HA
HA HA HA
CLAP CLAP
CLAP CLAP
HAHA HA HAHA!
CLAP
CLAP
DONATE

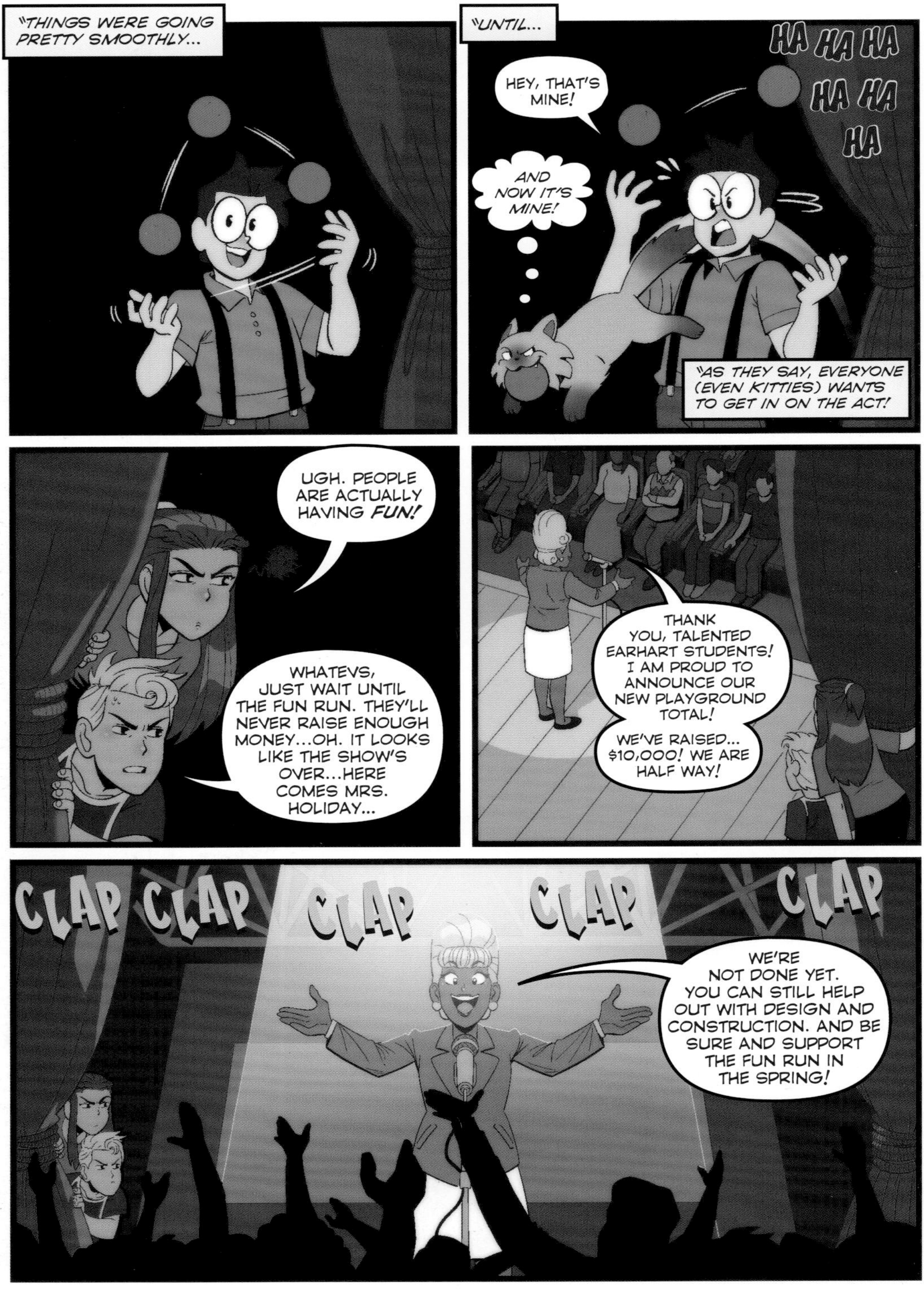
"THINGS WERE GOING PRETTY SMOOTHLY...
"UNTIL...
HA HA HA HA HA HA
HEY, THAT'S MINE!
AND NOW IT'S MINE!
"AS THEY SAY, EVERYONE (EVEN KITTIES) WANTS TO GET IN ON THE ACT!
UGH. PEOPLE ARE ACTUALLY HAVING *FUN!*
WHATEVS, JUST WAIT UNTIL THE FUN RUN. THEY'LL NEVER RAISE ENOUGH MONEY...OH. IT LOOKS LIKE THE SHOW'S OVER...HERE COMES MRS. HOLIDAY...
THANK YOU, TALENTED EARHART STUDENTS! I AM PROUD TO ANNOUNCE OUR NEW PLAYGROUND TOTAL!
WE'VE RAISED... $10,000! WE ARE HALF WAY!
CLAP CLAP CLAP CLAP CLAP
WE'RE NOT DONE YET. YOU CAN STILL HELP OUT WITH DESIGN AND CONSTRUCTION. AND BE SURE AND SUPPORT THE FUN RUN IN THE SPRING!

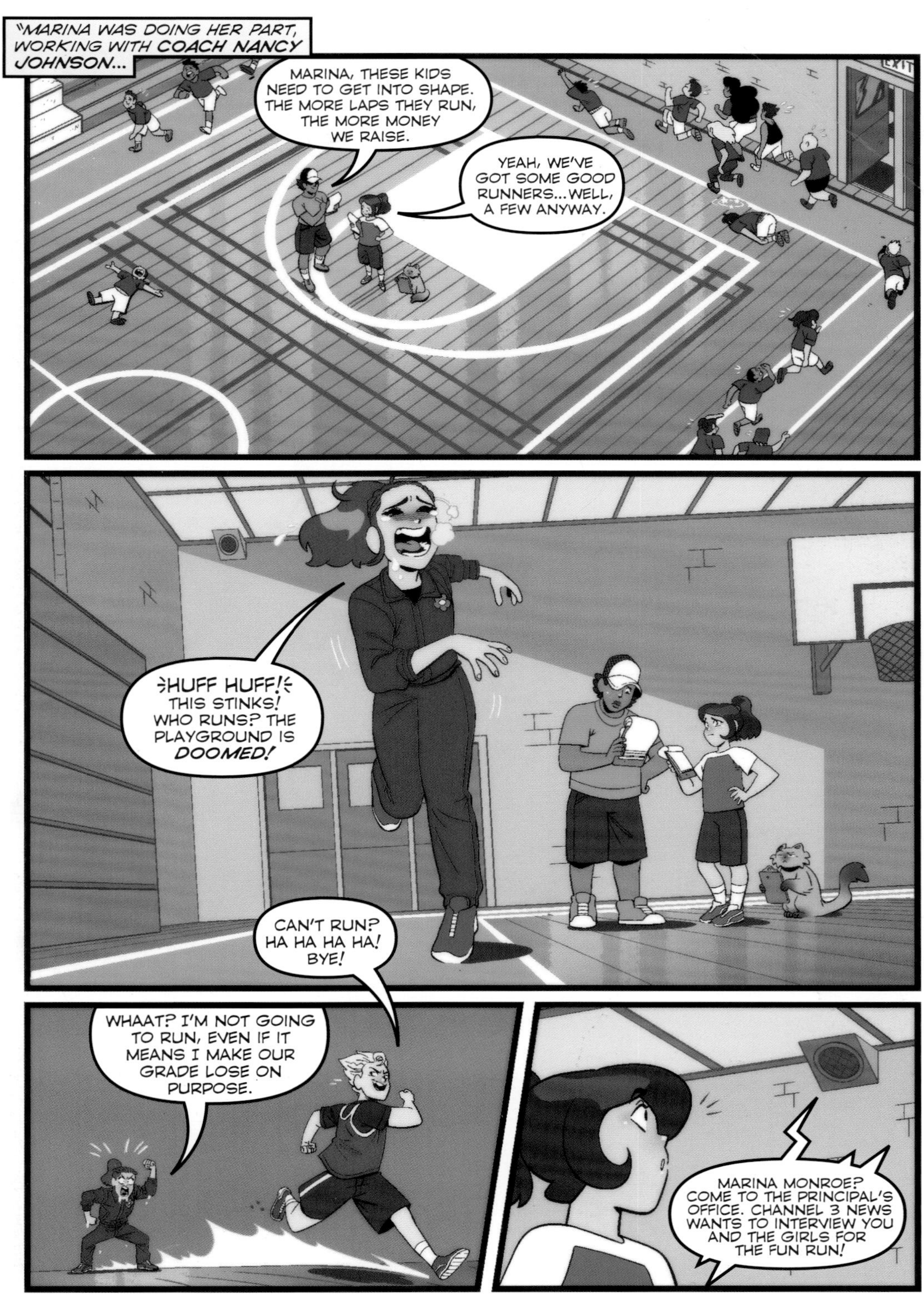
"MARINA WAS DOING HER PART, WORKING WITH COACH NANCY JOHNSON...
MARINA, THESE KIDS NEED TO GET INTO SHAPE. THE MORE LAPS THEY RUN, THE MORE MONEY WE RAISE.
YEAH, WE'VE GOT SOME GOOD RUNNERS...WELL, A FEW ANYWAY.
EXIT
HUFF HUFF! THIS STINKS! WHO RUNS? THE PLAYGROUND IS DOOMED!
CAN'T RUN? HA HA HA HA! BYE!
WHAAT? I'M NOT GOING TO RUN, EVEN IF IT MEANS I MAKE OUR GRADE LOSE ON PURPOSE.
MARINA MONROE? COME TO THE PRINCIPAL'S OFFICE. CHANNEL 3 NEWS WANTS TO INTERVIEW YOU AND THE GIRLS FOR THE FUN RUN!

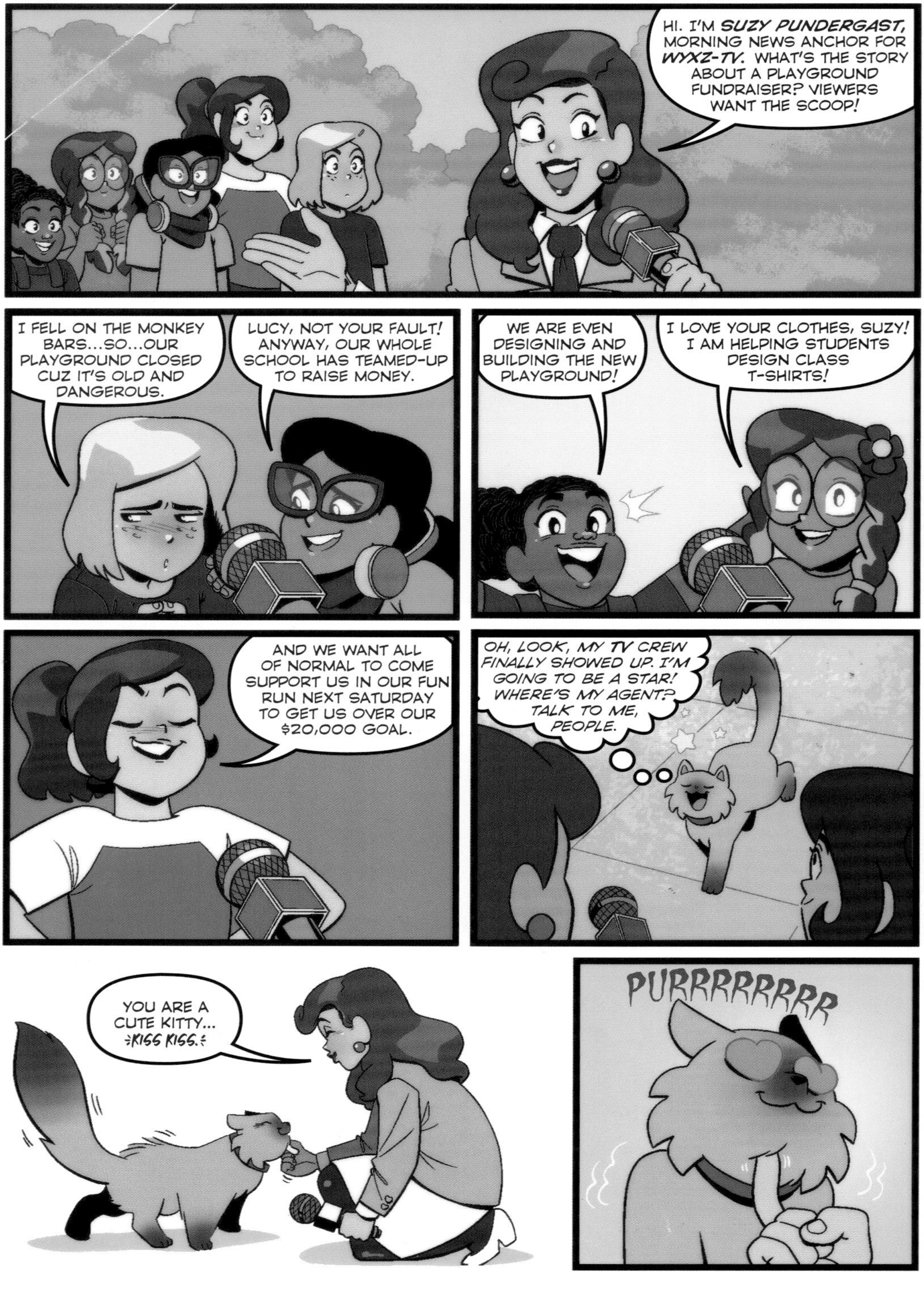
HI. I'M SUZY PUNDERGAST, MORNING NEWS ANCHOR FOR WYXZ-TV. WHAT'S THE STORY ABOUT A PLAYGROUND FUNDRAISER? VIEWERS WANT THE SCOOP!
I FELL ON THE MONKEY BARS...SO...OUR PLAYGROUND CLOSED CUZ IT'S OLD AND DANGEROUS.
LUCY, NOT YOUR FAULT! ANYWAY, OUR WHOLE SCHOOL HAS TEAMED-UP TO RAISE MONEY.
WE ARE EVEN DESIGNING AND BUILDING THE NEW PLAYGROUND!
I LOVE YOUR CLOTHES, SUZY! I AM HELPING STUDENTS DESIGN CLASS T-SHIRTS!
AND WE WANT ALL OF NORMAL TO COME SUPPORT US IN OUR FUN RUN NEXT SATURDAY TO GET US OVER OUR $20,000 GOAL.
OH, LOOK, MY TV CREW FINALLY SHOWED UP. I'M GOING TO BE A STAR! WHERE'S MY AGENT? TALK TO ME, PEOPLE.
YOU ARE A CUTE KITTY... KISS KISS.
PURRRRRRRR

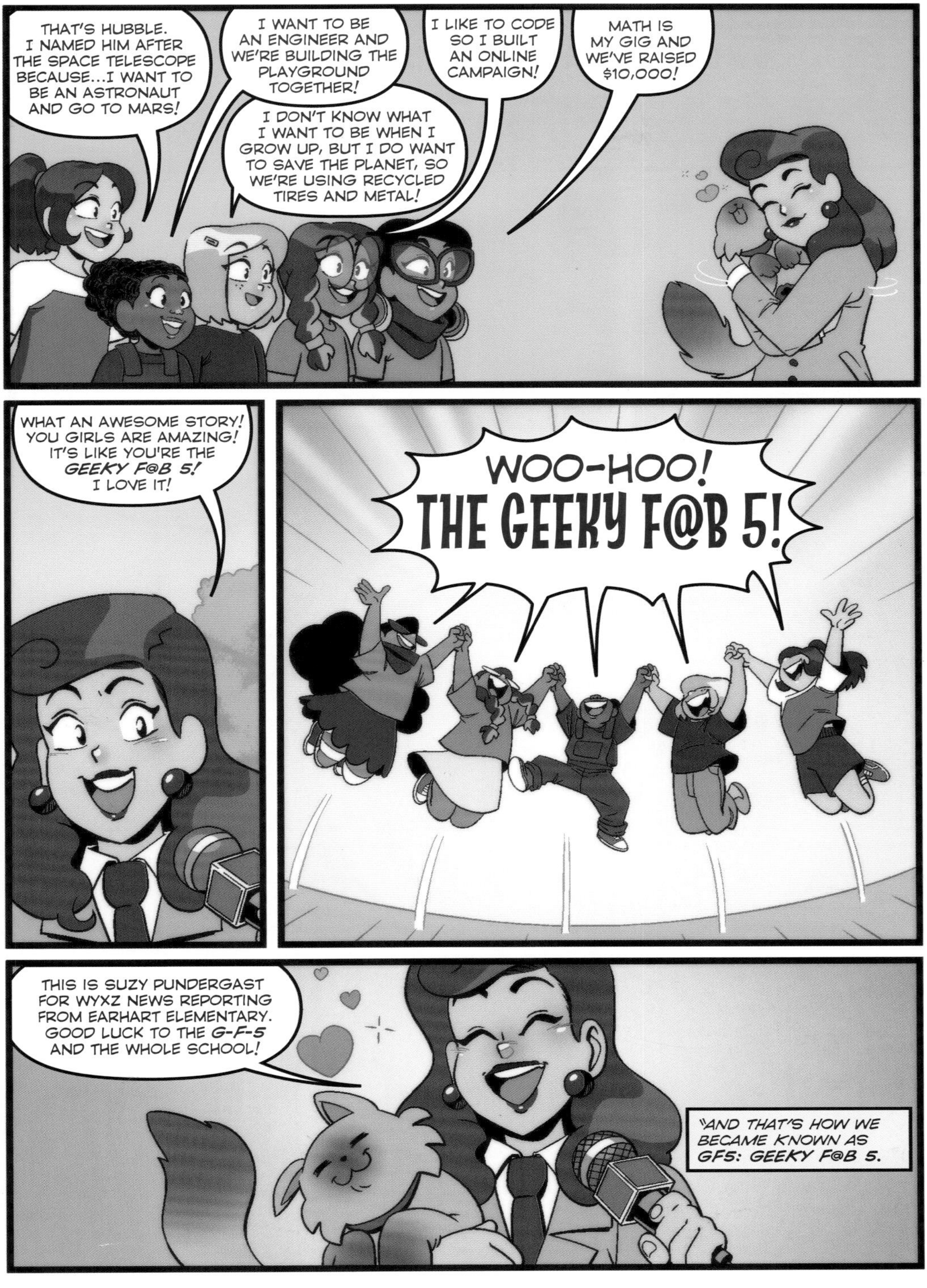
THAT'S HUBBLE. I NAMED HIM AFTER THE SPACE TELESCOPE BECAUSE...I WANT TO BE AN ASTRONAUT AND GO TO MARS!
I WANT TO BE AN ENGINEER AND WE'RE BUILDING THE PLAYGROUND TOGETHER!
I DON'T KNOW WHAT I WANT TO BE WHEN I GROW UP, BUT I DO WANT TO SAVE THE PLANET, SO WE'RE USING RECYCLED TIRES AND METAL!
I LIKE TO CODE SO I BUILT AN ONLINE CAMPAIGN!
MATH IS MY GIG AND WE'VE RAISED $10,000!
WHAT AN AWESOME STORY! YOU GIRLS ARE AMAZING! IT'S LIKE YOU'RE THE *GEEKY F@B 5!* I LOVE IT!
WOO-HOO! THE GEEKY F@B 5!
THIS IS SUZY PUNDERGAST FOR WYXZ NEWS REPORTING FROM EARHART ELEMENTARY. GOOD LUCK TO THE *G-F-5* AND THE WHOLE SCHOOL!
"AND THAT'S HOW WE BECAME KNOWN AS GF5: GEEKY F@B 5.

CHAPTER SEVEN: THE FUN RUN

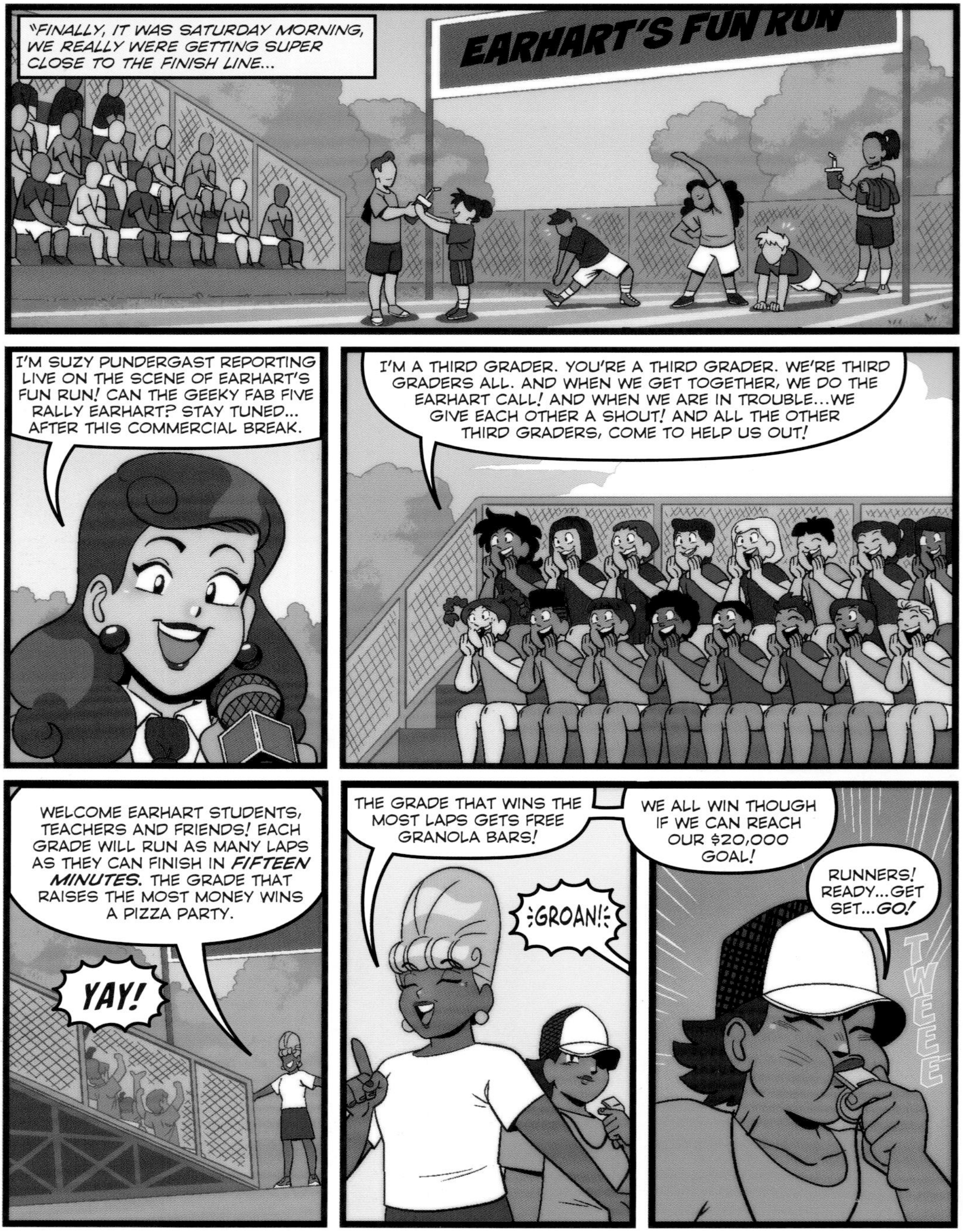

"FINALLY, IT WAS SATURDAY MORNING, WE REALLY WERE GETTING SUPER CLOSE TO THE FINISH LINE...
EARHART'S FUN RUN
I'M SUZY PUNDERGAST REPORTING LIVE ON THE SCENE OF EARHART'S FUN RUN! CAN THE GEEKY FAB FIVE RALLY EARHART? STAY TUNED... AFTER THIS COMMERCIAL BREAK.
I'M A THIRD GRADER. YOU'RE A THIRD GRADER. WE'RE THIRD GRADERS ALL. AND WHEN WE GET TOGETHER, WE DO THE EARHART CALL! AND WHEN WE ARE IN TROUBLE...WE GIVE EACH OTHER A SHOUT! AND ALL THE OTHER THIRD GRADERS, COME TO HELP US OUT!
WELCOME EARHART STUDENTS, TEACHERS AND FRIENDS! EACH GRADE WILL RUN AS MANY LAPS AS THEY CAN FINISH IN FIFTEEN MINUTES. THE GRADE THAT RAISES THE MOST MONEY WINS A PIZZA PARTY.
YAY!
THE GRADE THAT WINS THE MOST LAPS GETS FREE GRANOLA BARS!
GROAN!
WE ALL WIN THOUGH IF WE CAN REACH OUR $20,000 GOAL!
RUNNERS! READY...GET SET...GO!
TWEEE

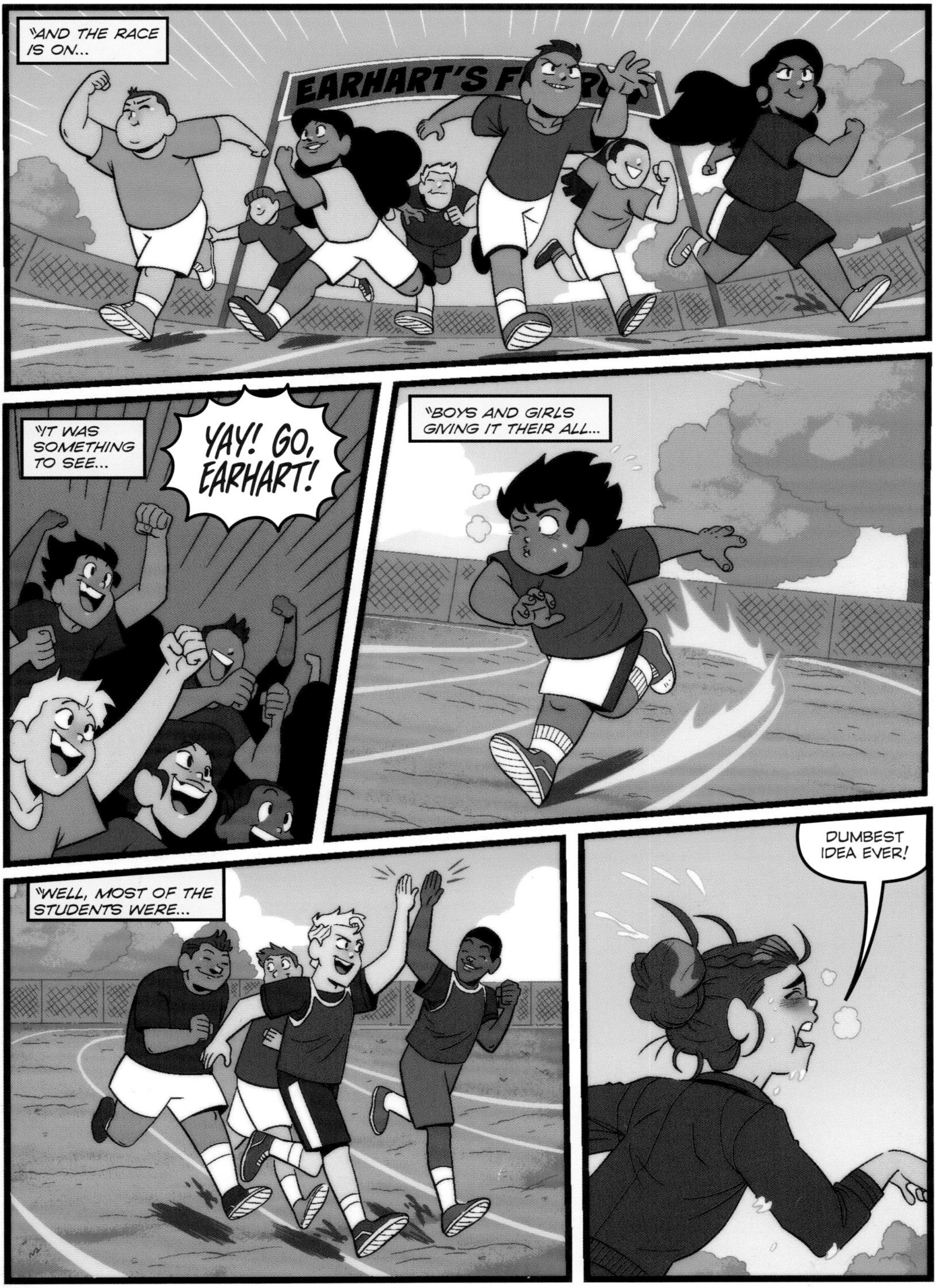
"AND THE RACE IS ON...
"IT WAS SOMETHING TO SEE...
YAY! GO, EARHART!
"BOYS AND GIRLS GIVING IT THEIR ALL...
"WELL, MOST OF THE STUDENTS WERE...
DUMBEST IDEA EVER!

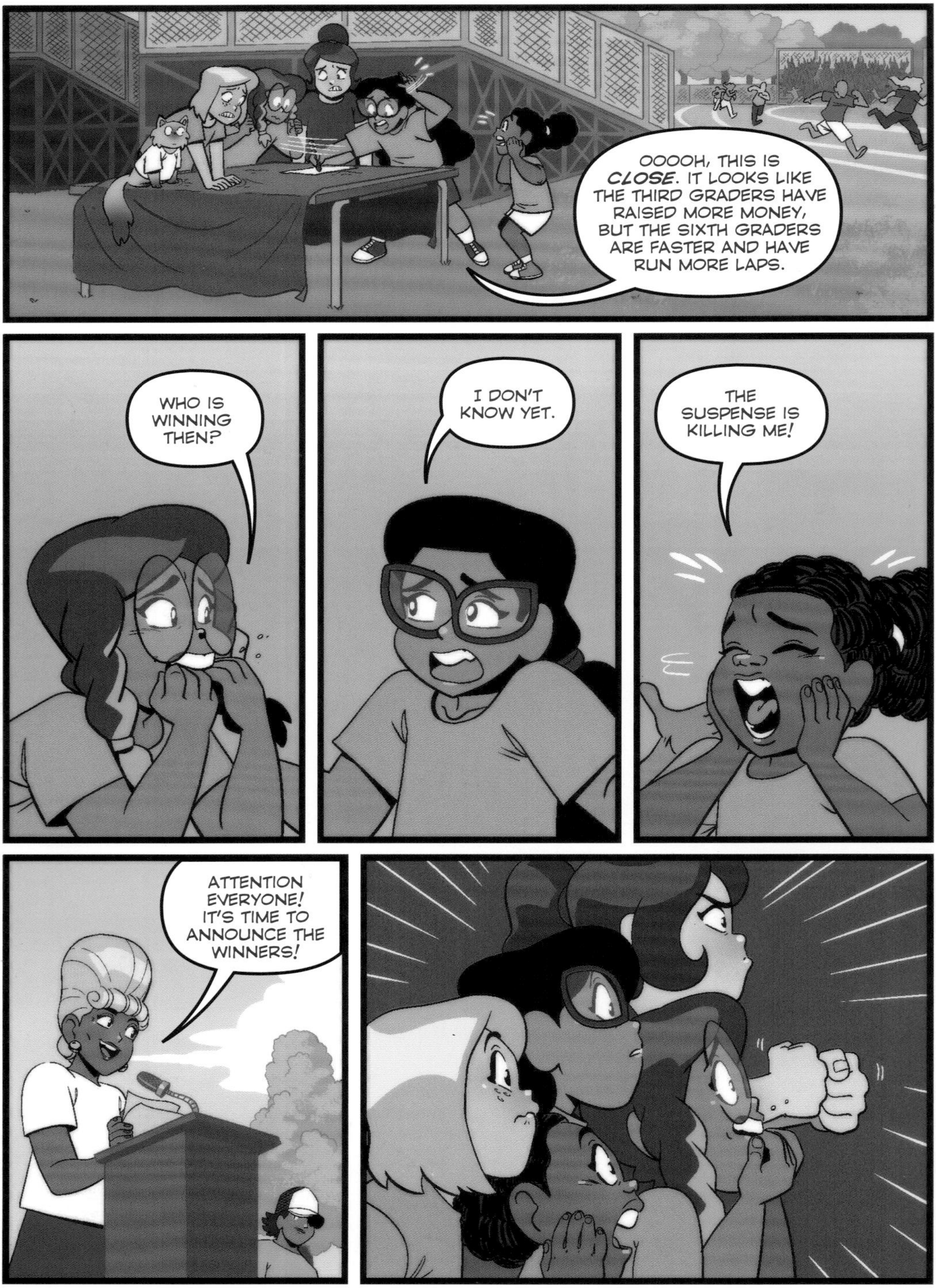
OOOOH, THIS IS CLOSE. IT LOOKS LIKE THE THIRD GRADERS HAVE RAISED MORE MONEY, BUT THE SIXTH GRADERS ARE FASTER AND HAVE RUN MORE LAPS.
WHO IS WINNING THEN?
I DON'T KNOW YET.
THE SUSPENSE IS KILLING ME!
ATTENTION EVERYONE! IT'S TIME TO ANNOUNCE THE WINNERS!

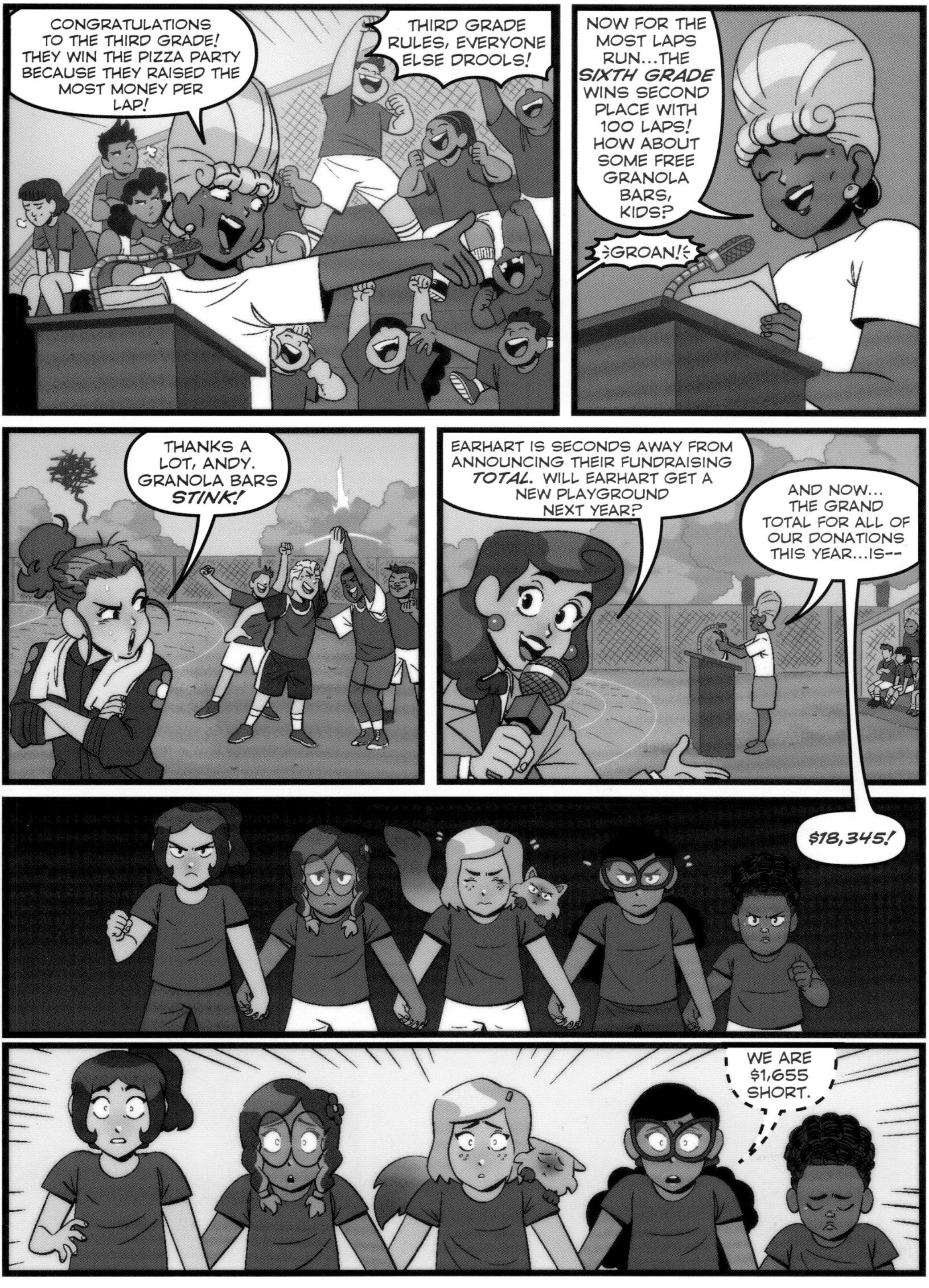
CONGRATULATIONS TO THE THIRD GRADE! THEY WIN THE PIZZA PARTY BECAUSE THEY RAISED THE MOST MONEY PER LAP!
THIRD GRADE RULES, EVERYONE ELSE DROOLS!
NOW FOR THE MOST LAPS RUN...THE SIXTH GRADE WINS SECOND PLACE WITH 100 LAPS! HOW ABOUT SOME FREE GRANOLA BARS, KIDS?
GROAN!
THANKS A LOT, ANDY. GRANOLA BARS STINK!
EARHART IS SECONDS AWAY FROM ANNOUNCING THEIR FUNDRAISING TOTAL. WILL EARHART GET A NEW PLAYGROUND NEXT YEAR?
AND NOW... THE GRAND TOTAL FOR ALL OF OUR DONATIONS THIS YEAR...IS--
$18,345!
WE ARE $1,655 SHORT.

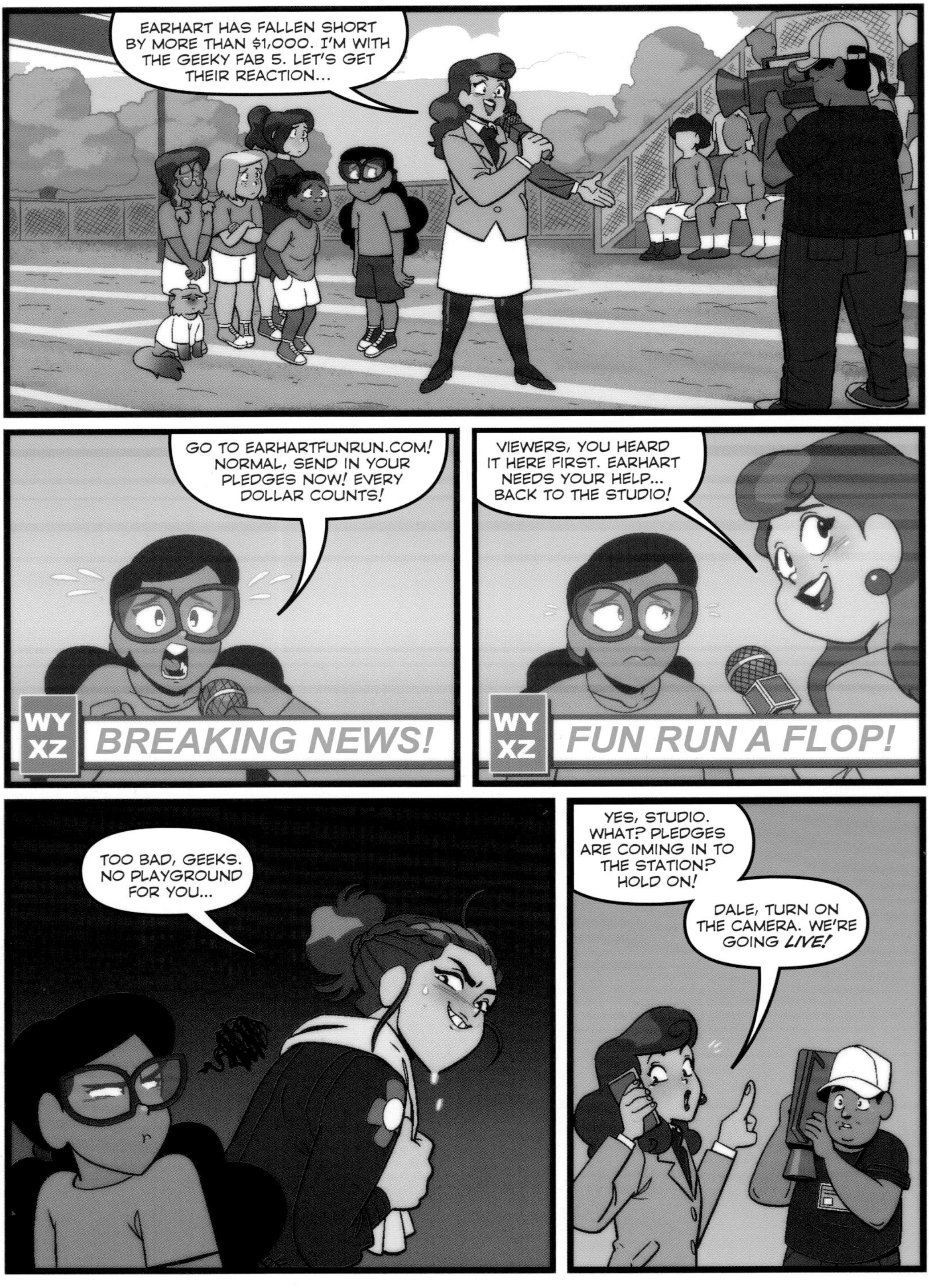
EARHART HAS FALLEN SHORT BY MORE THAN $1,000. I'M WITH THE GEEKY FAB 5. LET'S GET THEIR REACTION...
GO TO EARHARTFUNRUN.COM! NORMAL, SEND IN YOUR PLEDGES NOW! EVERY DOLLAR COUNTS!
WYXZ
BREAKING NEWS!
VIEWERS, YOU HEARD IT HERE FIRST. EARHART NEEDS YOUR HELP... BACK TO THE STUDIO!
WYXZ
FUN RUN A FLOP!
TOO BAD, GEEKS. NO PLAYGROUND FOR YOU...
YES, STUDIO. WHAT? PLEDGES ARE COMING IN TO THE STATION? HOLD ON!
DALE, TURN ON THE CAMERA. WE'RE GOING *LIVE!*

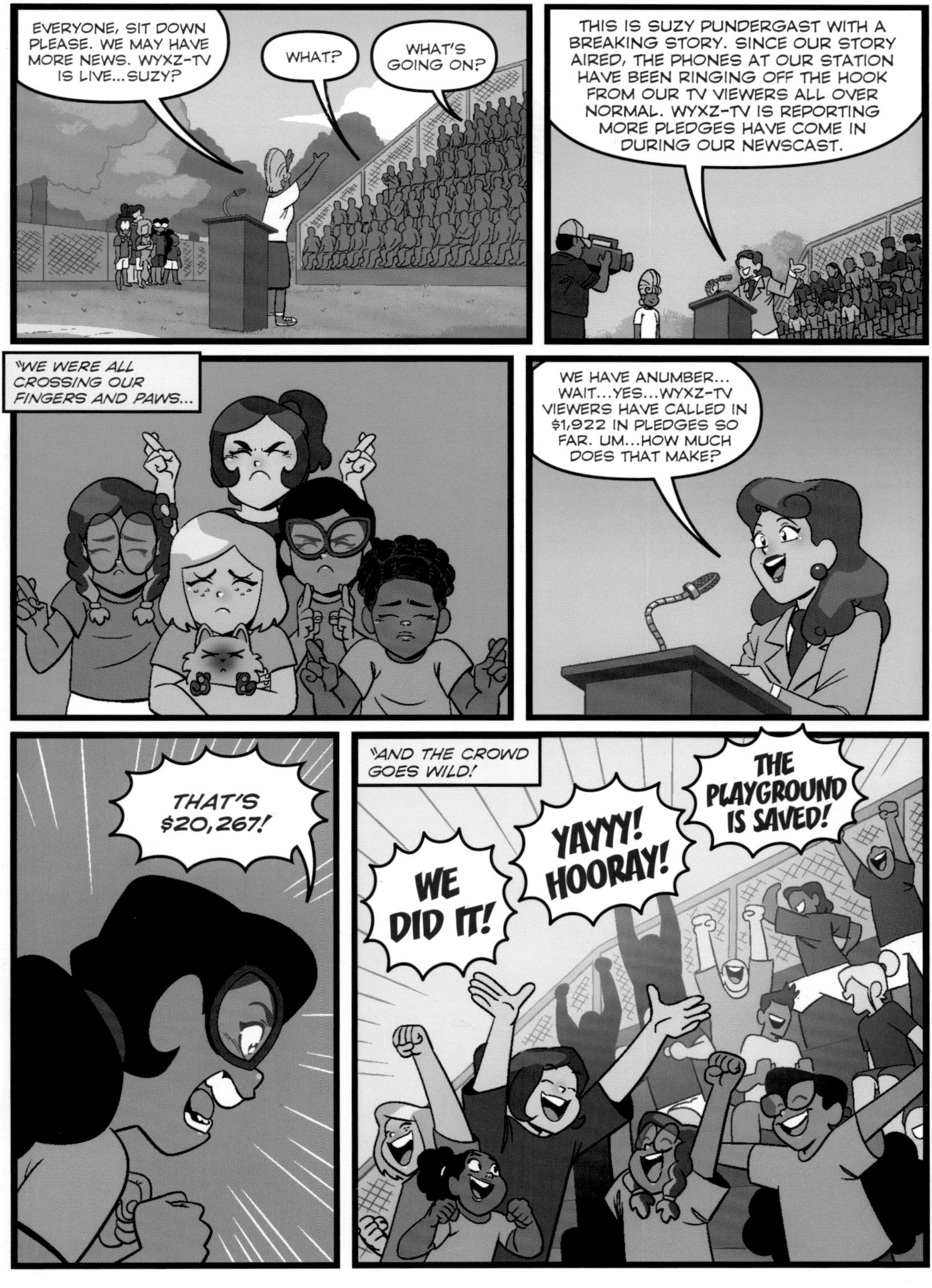
EVERYONE, SIT DOWN PLEASE. WE MAY HAVE MORE NEWS. WYXZ-TV IS LIVE...SUZY?
WHAT?
WHAT'S GOING ON?
THIS IS SUZY PUNDERGAST WITH A BREAKING STORY. SINCE OUR STORY AIRED, THE PHONES AT OUR STATION HAVE BEEN RINGING OFF THE HOOK FROM OUR TV VIEWERS ALL OVER NORMAL. WYXZ-TV IS REPORTING MORE PLEDGES HAVE COME IN DURING OUR NEWSCAST.
"WE WERE ALL CROSSING OUR FINGERS AND PAWS...
WE HAVE ANUMBER... WAIT...YES...WYXZ-TV VIEWERS HAVE CALLED IN $1,922 IN PLEDGES SO FAR. UM...HOW MUCH DOES THAT MAKE?
THAT'S $20,267!
"AND THE CROWD GOES WILD!
WE DID IT!
YAYYY! HOORAY!
THE PLAYGROUND IS SAVED!

CHAPTER EIGHT: EARHART SOARS AGAIN

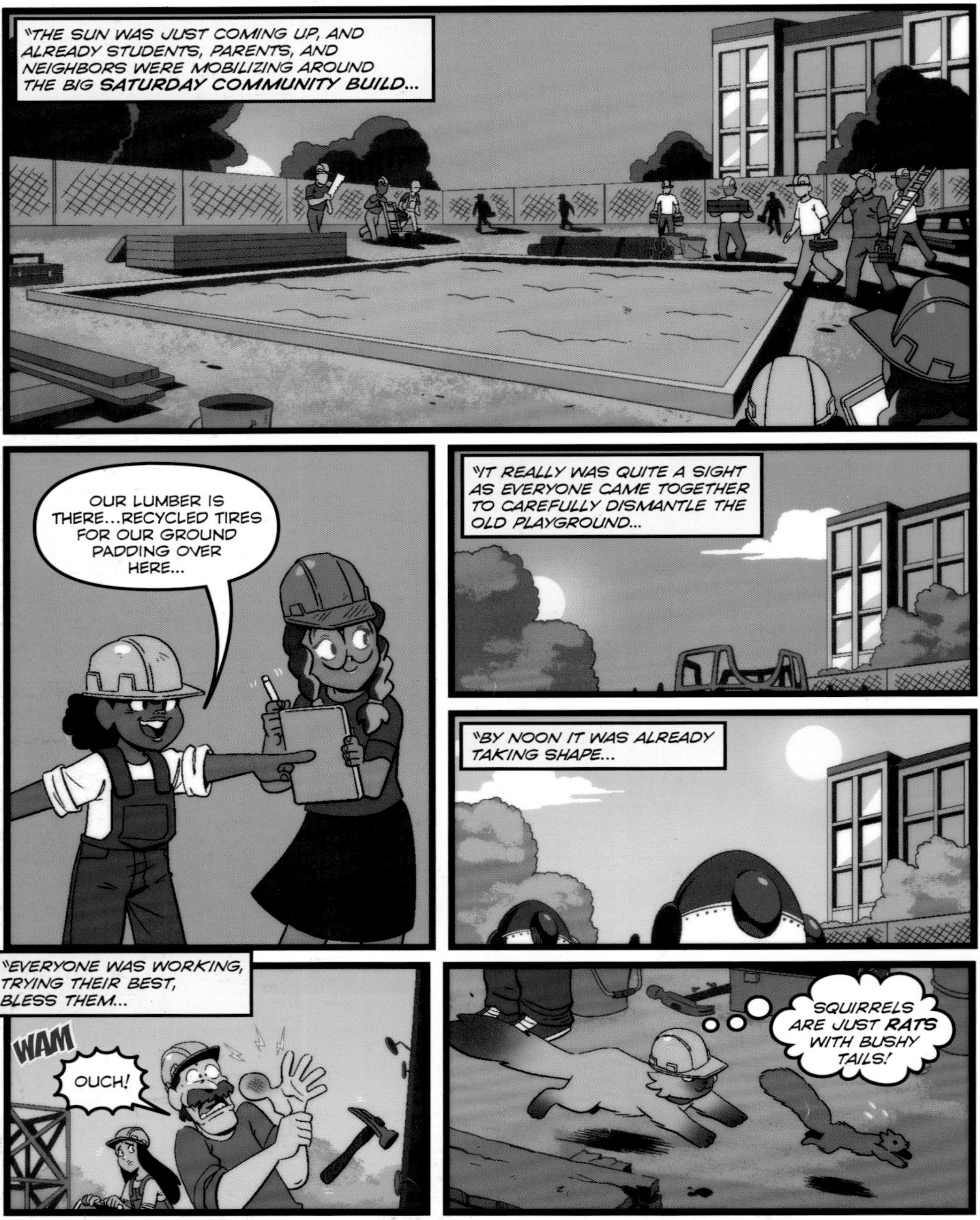

"THE SUN WAS JUST COMING UP, AND ALREADY STUDENTS, PARENTS, AND NEIGHBORS WERE MOBILIZING AROUND THE BIG SATURDAY COMMUNITY BUILD...
OUR LUMBER IS THERE...RECYCLED TIRES FOR OUR GROUND PADDING OVER HERE...
"IT REALLY WAS QUITE A SIGHT AS EVERYONE CAME TOGETHER TO CAREFULLY DISMANTLE THE OLD PLAYGROUND...
"BY NOON IT WAS ALREADY TAKING SHAPE...
"EVERYONE WAS WORKING, TRYING THEIR BEST, BLESS THEM...
WAM
OUCH!
SQUIRRELS ARE JUST RATS WITH BUSHY TAILS!

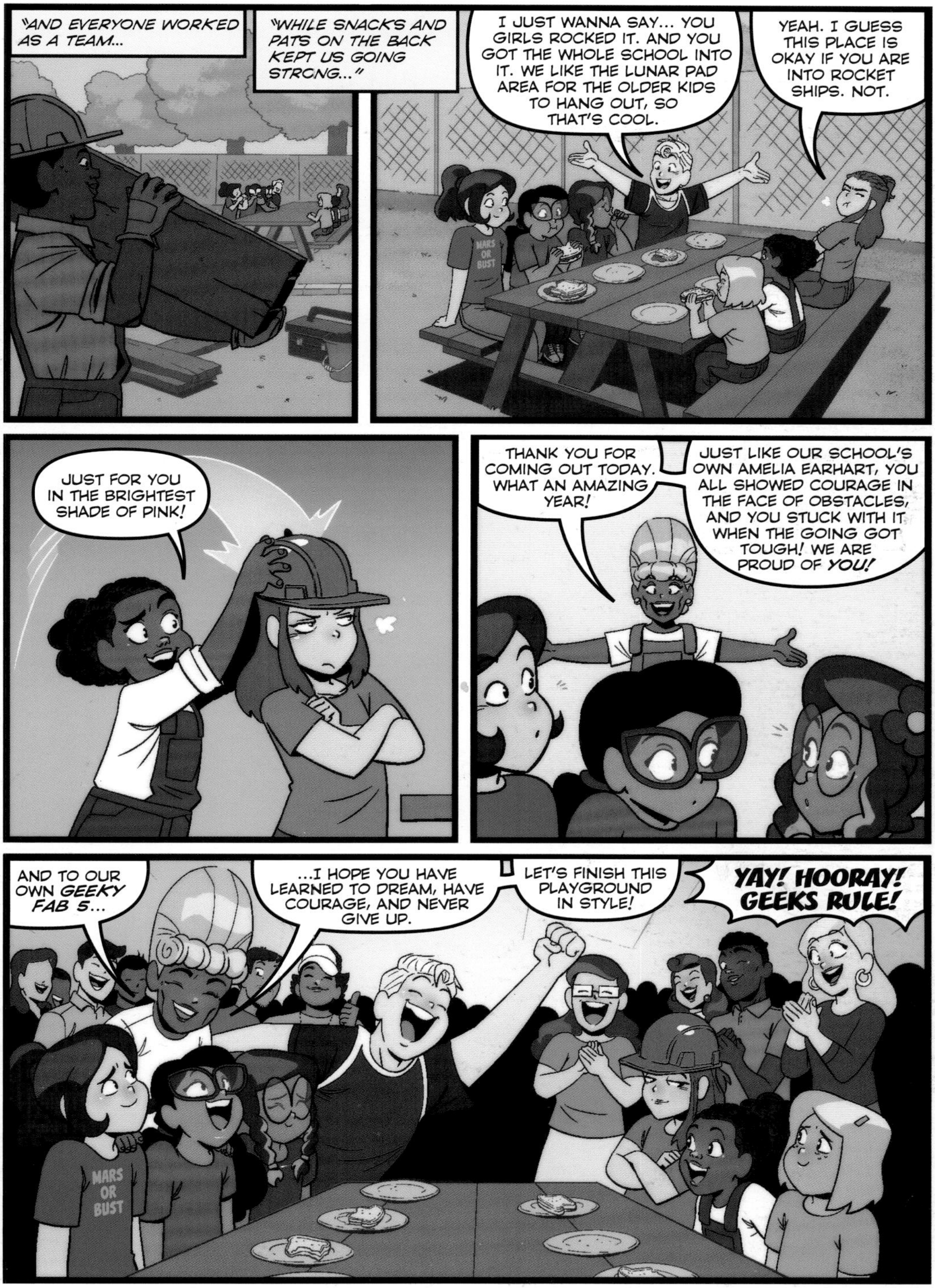
"AND EVERYONE WORKED AS A TEAM...
"WHILE SNACKS AND PATS ON THE BACK KEPT US GOING STRONG..."
I JUST WANNA SAY... YOU GIRLS ROCKED IT. AND YOU GOT THE WHOLE SCHOOL INTO IT. WE LIKE THE LUNAR PAD AREA FOR THE OLDER KIDS TO HANG OUT, SO THAT'S COOL.
YEAH. I GUESS THIS PLACE IS OKAY IF YOU ARE INTO ROCKET SHIPS. NOT.
MARS OR BUST
JUST FOR YOU IN THE BRIGHTEST SHADE OF PINK!
THANK YOU FOR COMING OUT TODAY. WHAT AN AMAZING YEAR!
JUST LIKE OUR SCHOOL'S OWN AMELIA EARHART, YOU ALL SHOWED COURAGE IN THE FACE OF OBSTACLES, AND YOU STUCK WITH IT WHEN THE GOING GOT TOUGH! WE ARE PROUD OF *YOU!*
AND TO OUR OWN *GEEKY FAB 5*...
...I HOPE YOU HAVE LEARNED TO DREAM, HAVE COURAGE, AND NEVER GIVE UP.
LET'S FINISH THIS PLAYGROUND IN STYLE!
YAY! HOORAY! GEEKS RULE!
MARS OR BUST

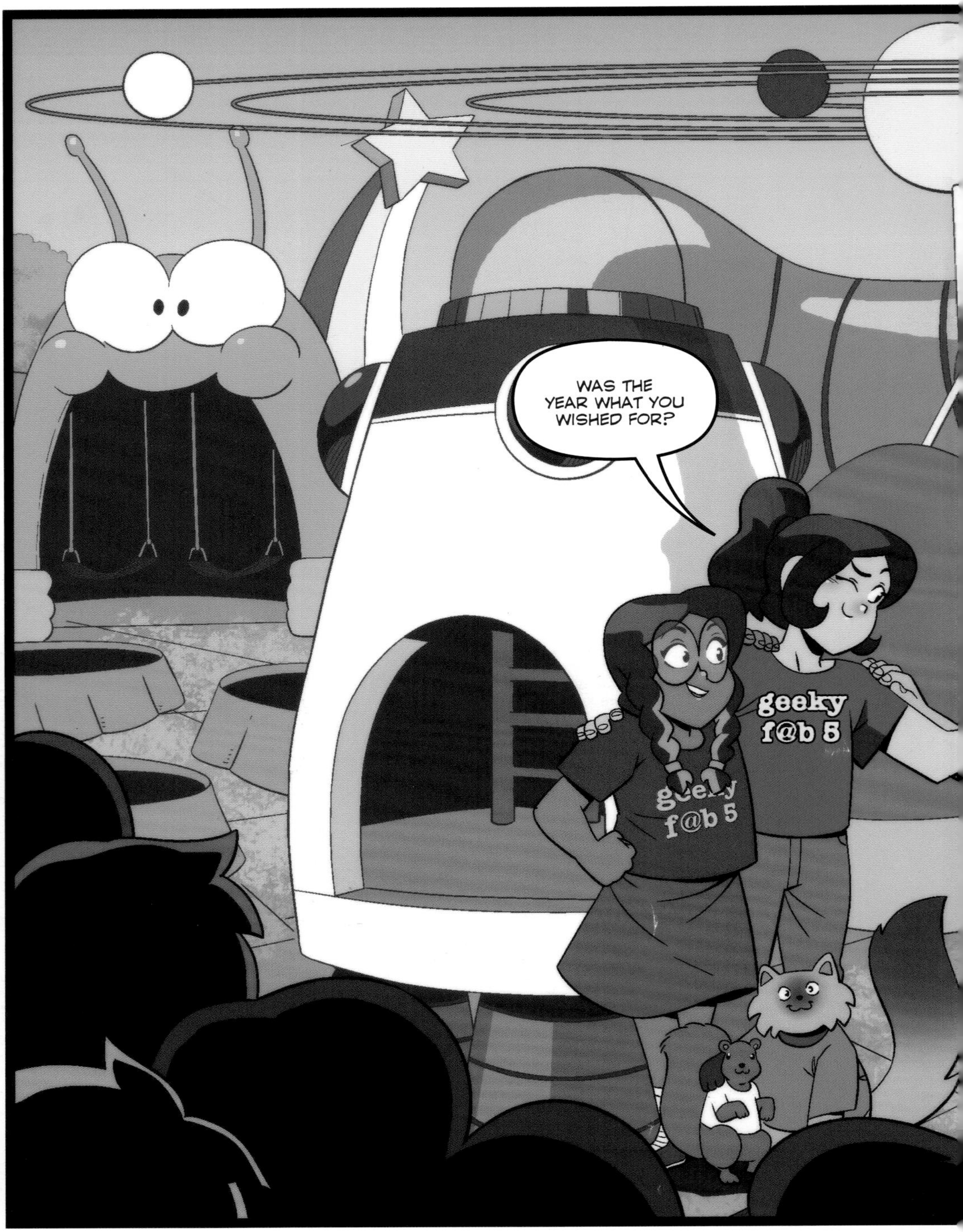
WAS THE YEAR WHAT YOU WISHED FOR?
geeky f@b 5
geeky f@b 5

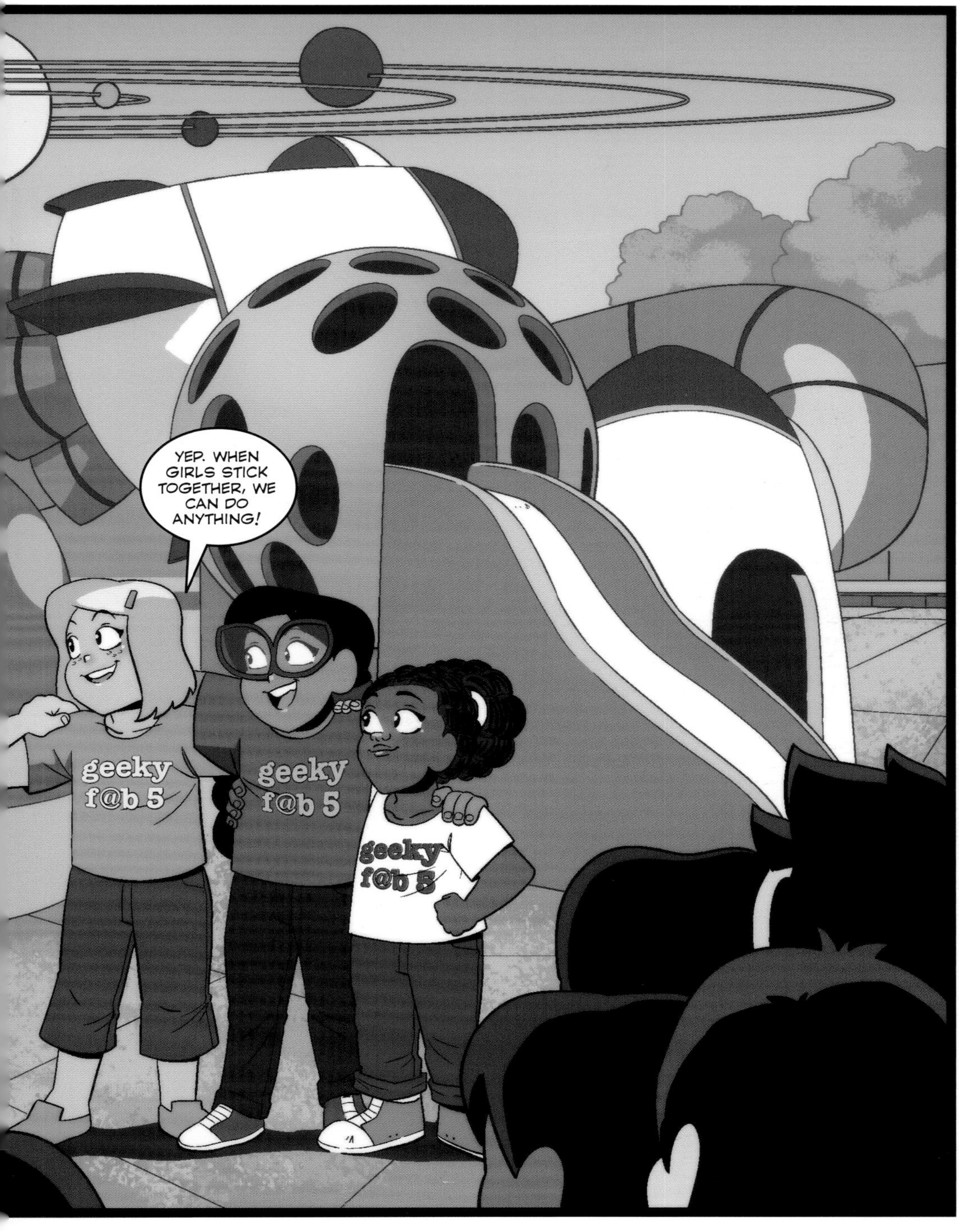
YEP. WHEN GIRLS STICK TOGETHER, WE CAN DO ANYTHING!
geeky f@b 5
geeky f@b 5
geeky f@b 5

WATCH OUT FOR PAPERCUTZ

Welcome to GEEKY F@B 5 #1 "It's Not Rocket Science," by Lucy & Liz Lareau, writers, and Ryan Jampole, artist. If you've picked up any Papercutz graphic novels before, you'll know that this is the page where I talk about behind-the-scenes Papercutz stuff. This time is a little different, as writer Lucy Lareau asked if she could talk to you too. Well, I can't say no to either Lucy or Liz, so, here's Lucy...

Hi, Everyone!
My name is Lucy Lareau and I'm 12 years-old. That picture is really me and my two cool book dudes from Papercutz, the company dedicated to publishing great graphic novels for all ages. They helped me and my mom with this book. Jim Salicrup is the Editor-in-Chief, on the right, and Jeff Whitman is the Assistant Managing Editor, on the left. They work in New York City, which is far away from my home in the Illinois cornfields.

I had a blast creating a fun bunch of girls who are smart, kind, and who solve all kinds of problems in their school. Hubble, the snarky cat, is super fluffy and he is practically everyone's favorite character! Yes, Hubble is REAL and he is way too fuzzy and only likes to sleep on my brother's bed...unless he is in his basket on top of the fridge! You can see real pictures of Hubble at my website: geekyfabfive.com
I am writing these books because girls can change the world, especially when we stick together. Do you ever notice some of your classmates say "I can't"? I do it, too. Why? Sometimes I'm scared. Sometimes I'm afraid to make a mistake. But we really CAN do math. We CAN invent. We CAN run a mile or more. We CAN come up with good ideas and make a difference. Right, Jim? I mean, come on, people!

That's right, Lucy. I have a daughter and I would tell her all the time she should follow her dreams.

Did you notice in the book we talked about some really amazing women in history that proved girls dreams come true? Check them out!

Amelia Earhart: Amelia Earhart was a female airplane pilot and the first woman to fly solo across the Atlantic Ocean. She also wrote books and inspired other women pilots. In 1937, she attempted to fly around the world, but her plane disappeared and was lost over the Pacific Ocean. She was never found, but her courage inspired generations of women to pursue careers in aviation and aeronautical engineering.

Valentina Tereshkova: Valentina Tereshkova, who is from Russia, became the first woman to fly in space in 1963. The Russian word for astronaut is "cosmonaut." After four space flights, Valentina became a politician in Russia and represented her country as the head of the Soviet Committee for Women at the United Nations. She also said she would like to travel to Mars!

Sally Ride: Sally Ride was the first American woman to fly in space. In 1983, she flew on a space shuttle mission. As a space pioneer, she loved science and before she became an astronaut, attended college and dreamed of becoming an astrophysicist who studies the stars. After her career at NASA, she taught at the University of California in San Diego and mentored women and girls studying science and math.

Ready for more geeky f@b 5 fun? In their next adventure, the girls discover a hidden garden filled with monarch butterflies and honeybees. While they learn in science that monarchs and bees are becoming endangered, something threatens to destroy their secret butterfly garden behind Earhart. To solve the mystery, Hubble the GF5 mascot discovers a secret that gets him catnapped! In a race against time, the girls must rescue Hubble, save the garden, and solve "The Mystery of the Missing Monarchs." Stay tuned!

While everyone's eagerly waiting for the next GEEKY F@B 5 graphic novel, allow me to mention another STEM (Science, Technology, Engineering, and Math) inspired graphic novel from Papercutz: DINOSAUR EXPLORERS. Join Sean, Emily, Stone, and Rain, as they travel back in time with Dr. Da Vinci, Diana, and Starz (a robot), to discover everything there is to know about prehistoric life. It's a fun new series, and you can get a sneak preview of the first graphic novel on the following pages.

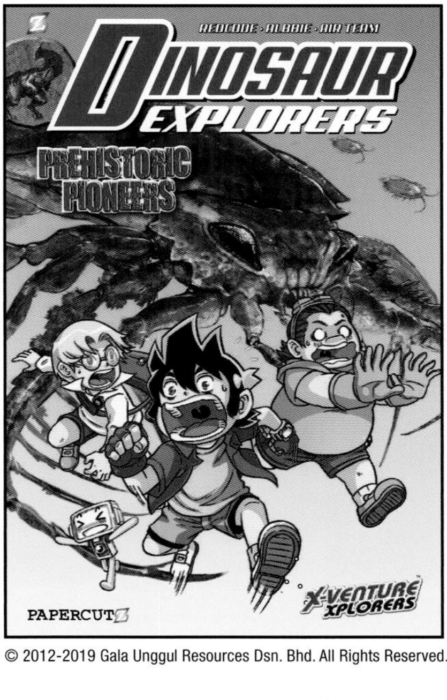
DINOSAUR EXPLORERS
PREHISTORIC PIONEERS
PAPERCUTZ
X-VENTURE XPLORERS

So, that about wraps up the premiere of GEEKY F@B 5. I'm sure Lucy, not to mention Liz, Ryan, and everyone else at Papercutz, is eager to find out what YOU thought of this graphic novel. Please use the contacts below to tell us, we really want to know!

Thanks,
Lucy and Jim

STAY IN TOUCH!

EMAIL:	salicrup@papercutz.com
WEB:	papercutz.com
TWITTER:	@papercutzgn
INSTAGRAM:	@papercutzgn
FACEBOOK:	PAPERCUTZGRAPHICNOVELS
FAN MAIL:	Papercutz, 160 Broadway, Suite 700, East Wing, New York, NY 10038

Special Preview of DINOSAUR EXPLORERS #1 "Prehistoric Pioneers" by Redcode, Albbie, and Air Team...

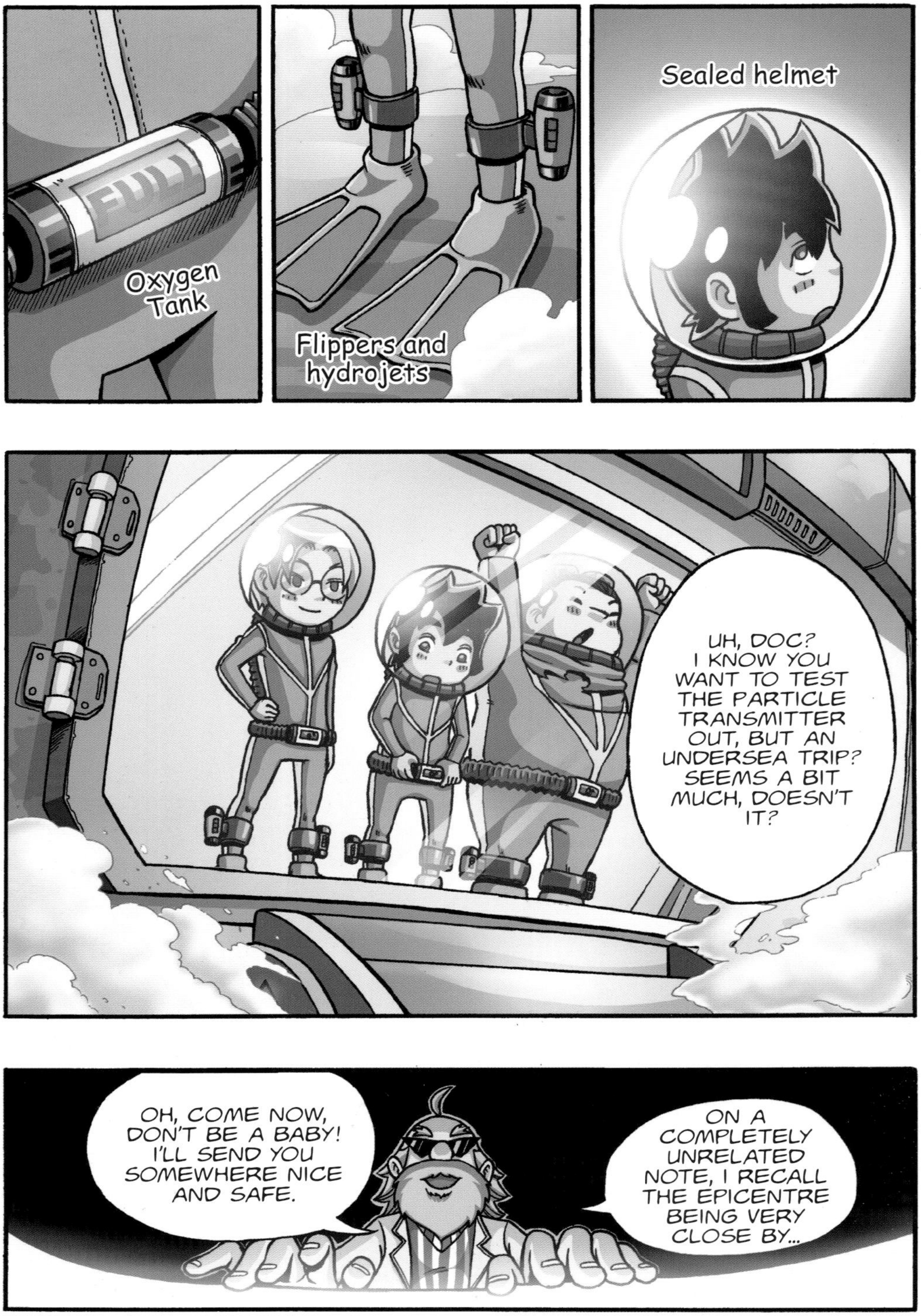
FULL
Oxygen Tank
Flippers and hydrojets
Sealed helmet
UH, DOC? I KNOW YOU WANT TO TEST THE PARTICLE TRANSMITTER OUT, BUT AN UNDERSEA TRIP? SEEMS A BIT MUCH, DOESN'T IT?
OH, COME NOW, DON'T BE A BABY! I'LL SEND YOU SOMEWHERE NICE AND SAFE.
ON A COMPLETELY UNRELATED NOTE, I RECALL THE EPICENTRE BEING VERY CLOSE BY...

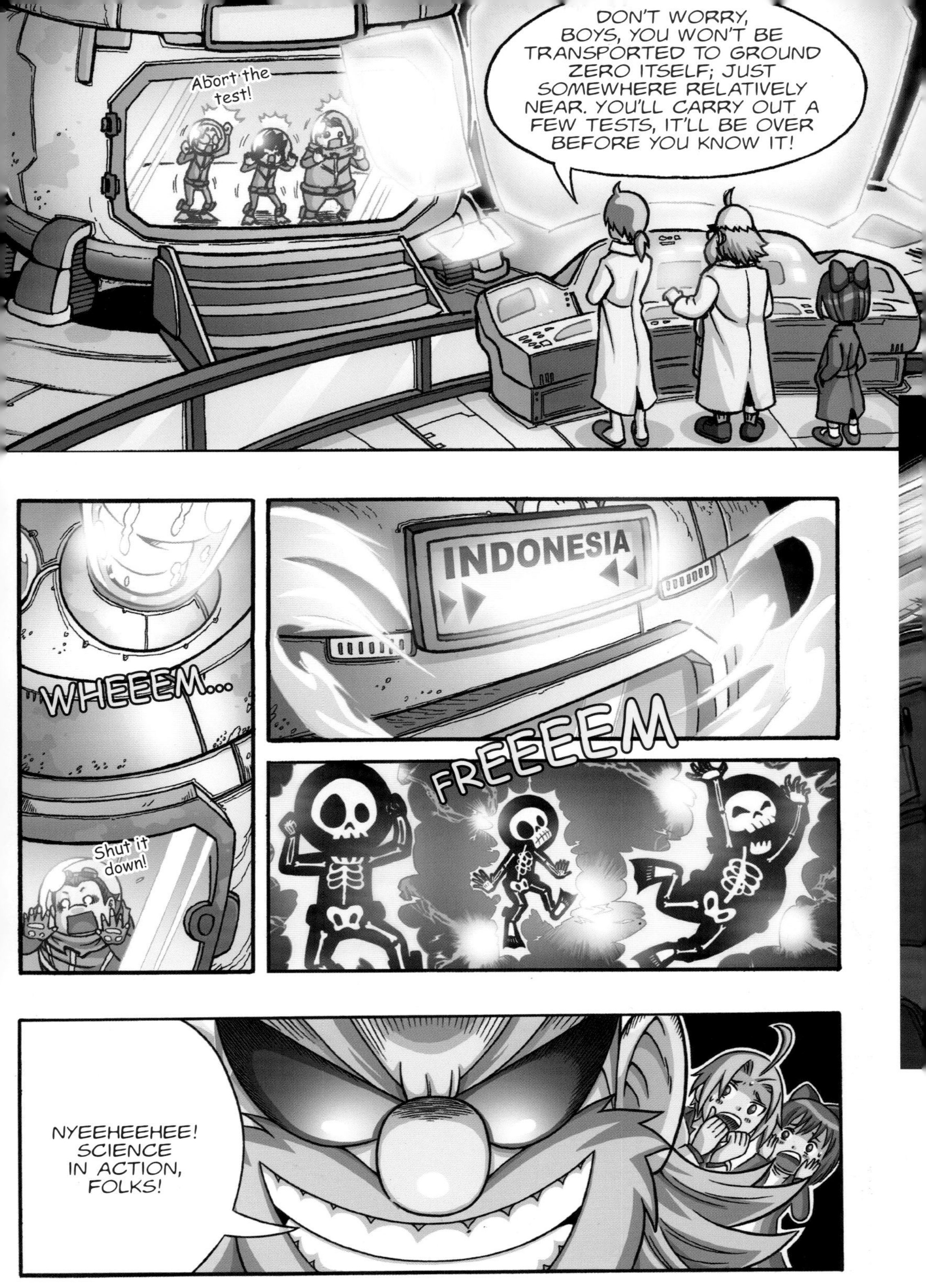
DON'T WORRY, BOYS, YOU WON'T BE TRANSPORTED TO GROUND ZERO ITSELF; JUST SOMEWHERE RELATIVELY NEAR. YOU'LL CARRY OUT A FEW TESTS, IT'LL BE OVER BEFORE YOU KNOW IT!
Abort the test!
WHEEEEM...
Shut it down!
INDONESIA
FREEEEEM
NYEEHEEHEE! SCIENCE IN ACTION, FOLKS!

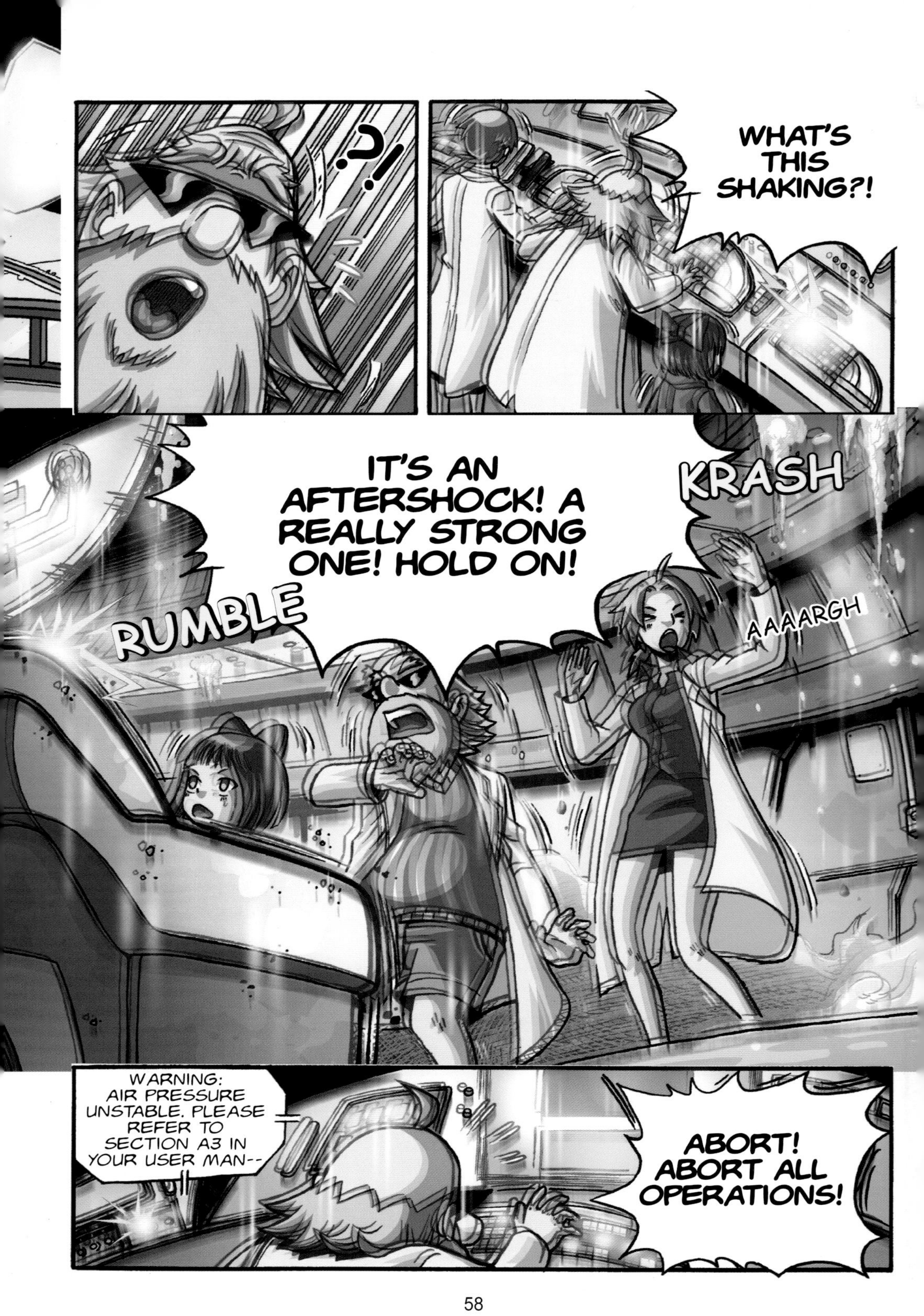

?!
WHAT'S THIS SHAKING?!
IT'S AN AFTERSHOCK! A REALLY STRONG ONE! HOLD ON!
KRASH
RUMBLE
AAAARGH
WARNING: AIR PRESSURE UNSTABLE. PLEASE REFER TO SECTION A3 IN YOUR USER MAN--
ABORT! ABORT ALL OPERATIONS!

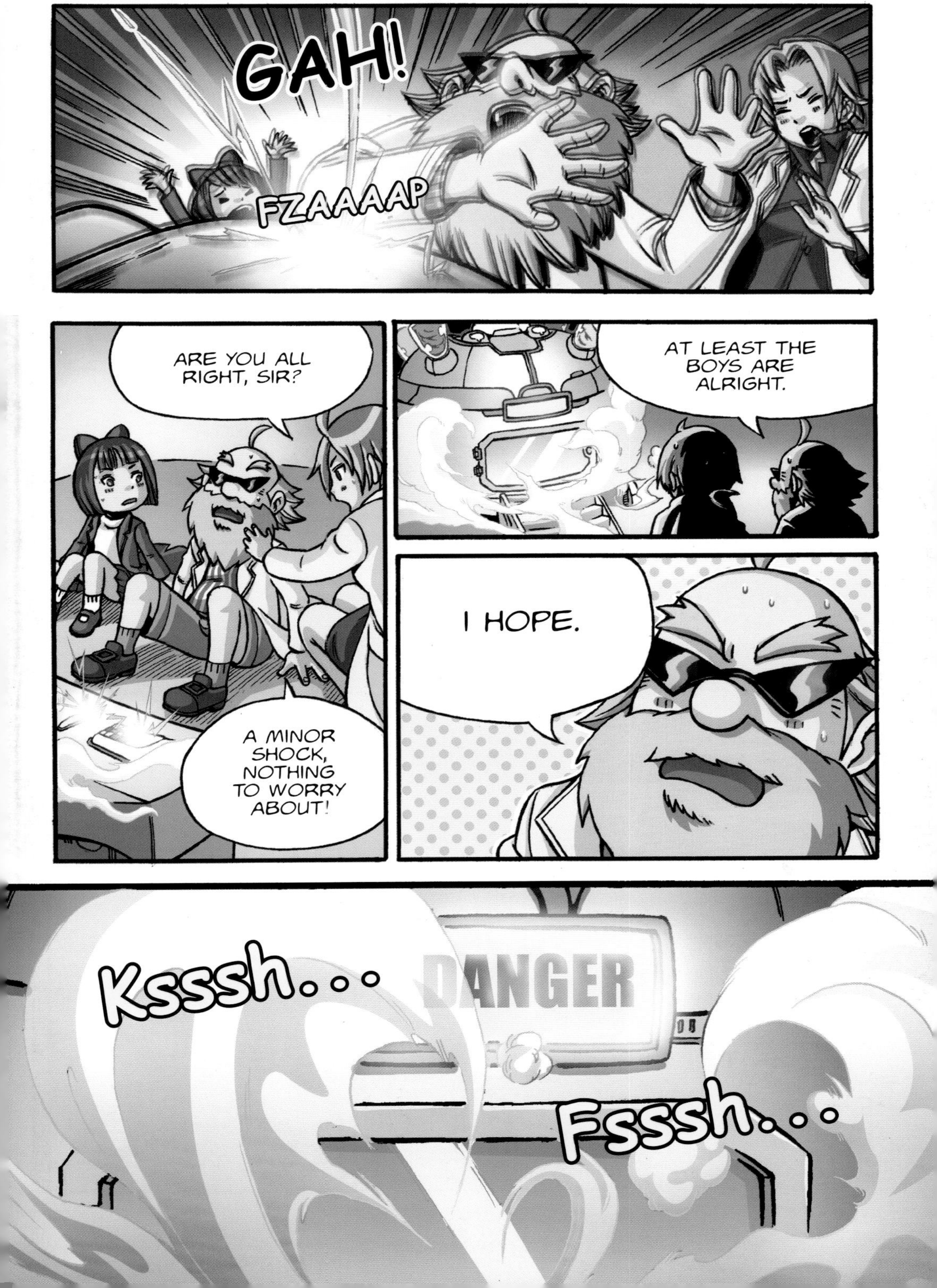
GAH!
FZAAAAP
ARE YOU ALL RIGHT, SIR?
A MINOR SHOCK, NOTHING TO WORRY ABOUT!
AT LEAST THE BOYS ARE ALRIGHT.
I HOPE.
Ksssh...
DANGER
Fsssh...

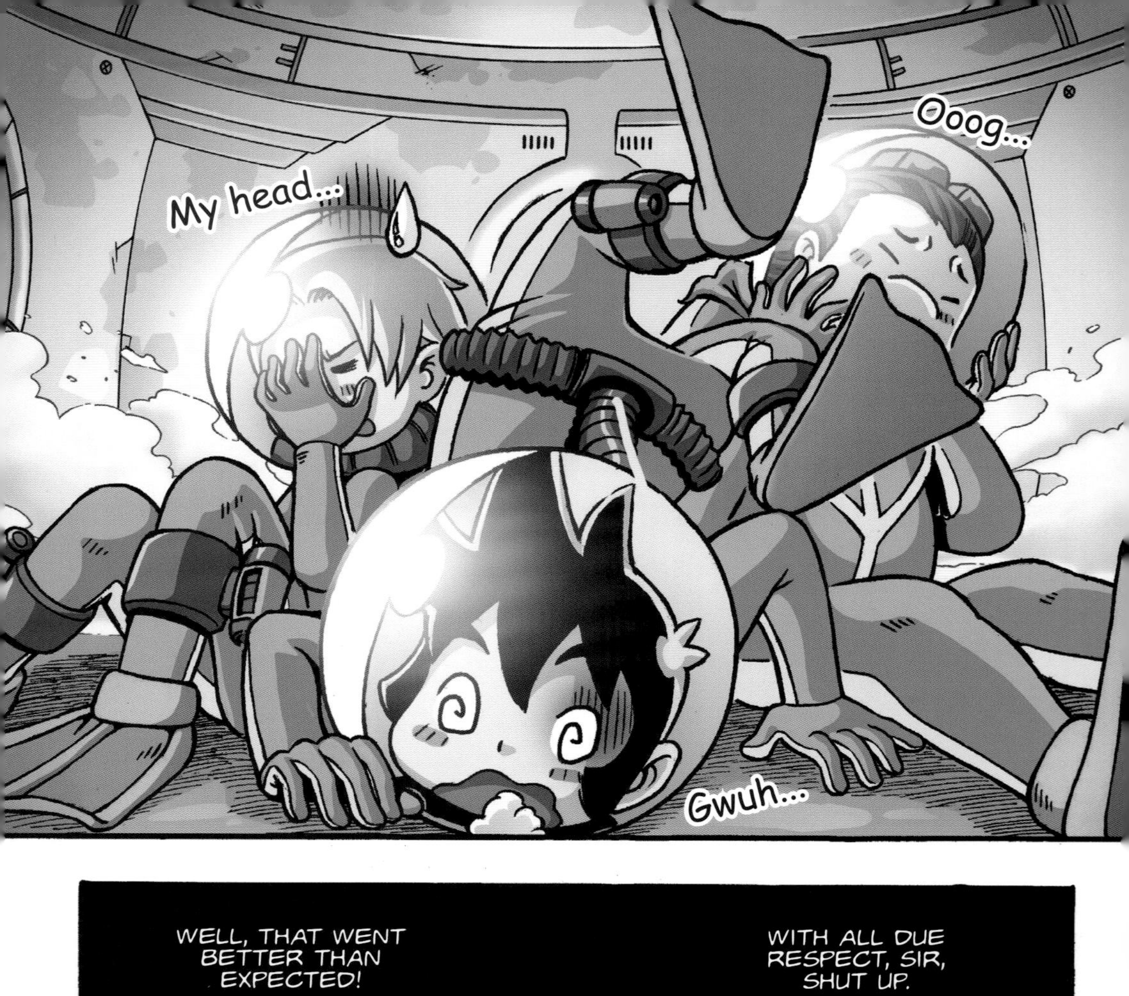
My head...
Ooog...
Gwuh...
WELL, THAT WENT BETTER THAN EXPECTED!
WITH ALL DUE RESPECT, SIR, SHUT UP.
Fzzzt
Shuff...
Plink
Fzzap

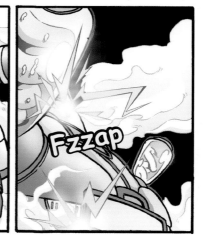

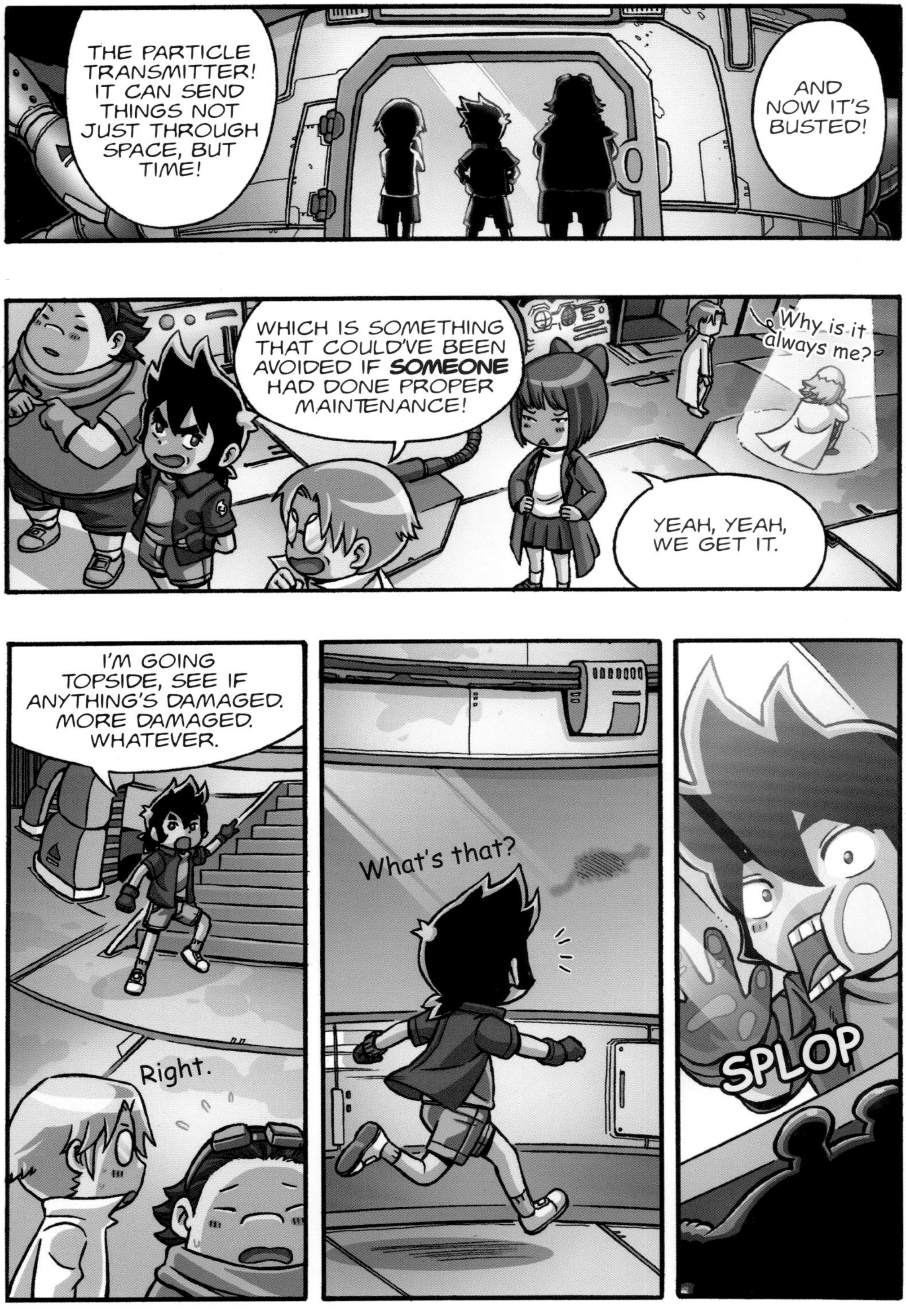

THE PARTICLE TRANSMITTER! IT CAN SEND THINGS NOT JUST THROUGH SPACE, BUT TIME!
AND NOW IT'S BUSTED!
WHICH IS SOMETHING THAT COULD'VE BEEN AVOIDED IF **SOMEONE** HAD DONE PROPER MAINTENANCE!
Why is it always me?
YEAH, YEAH, WE GET IT.
I'M GOING TOPSIDE, SEE IF ANYTHING'S DAMAGED. MORE DAMAGED. WHATEVER.
Right.
What's that?
SPLOP

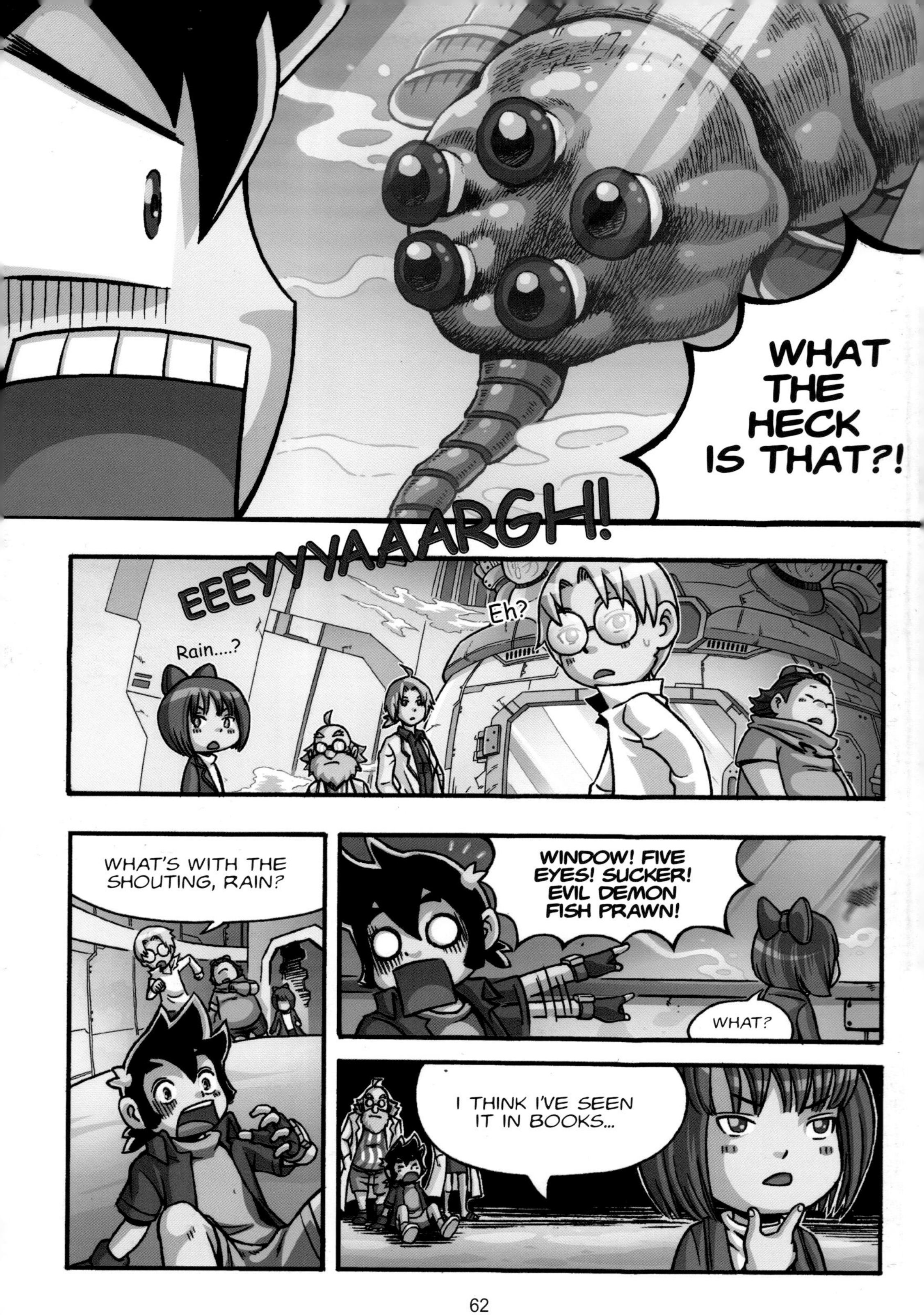
WHAT THE HECK IS THAT?!
EEEYYYAAAARGH!
Rain....?
Eh?
WHAT'S WITH THE SHOUTING, RAIN?
WINDOW! FIVE EYES! SUCKER! EVIL DEMON FISH PRAWN!
WHAT?
I THINK I'VE SEEN IT IN BOOKS...

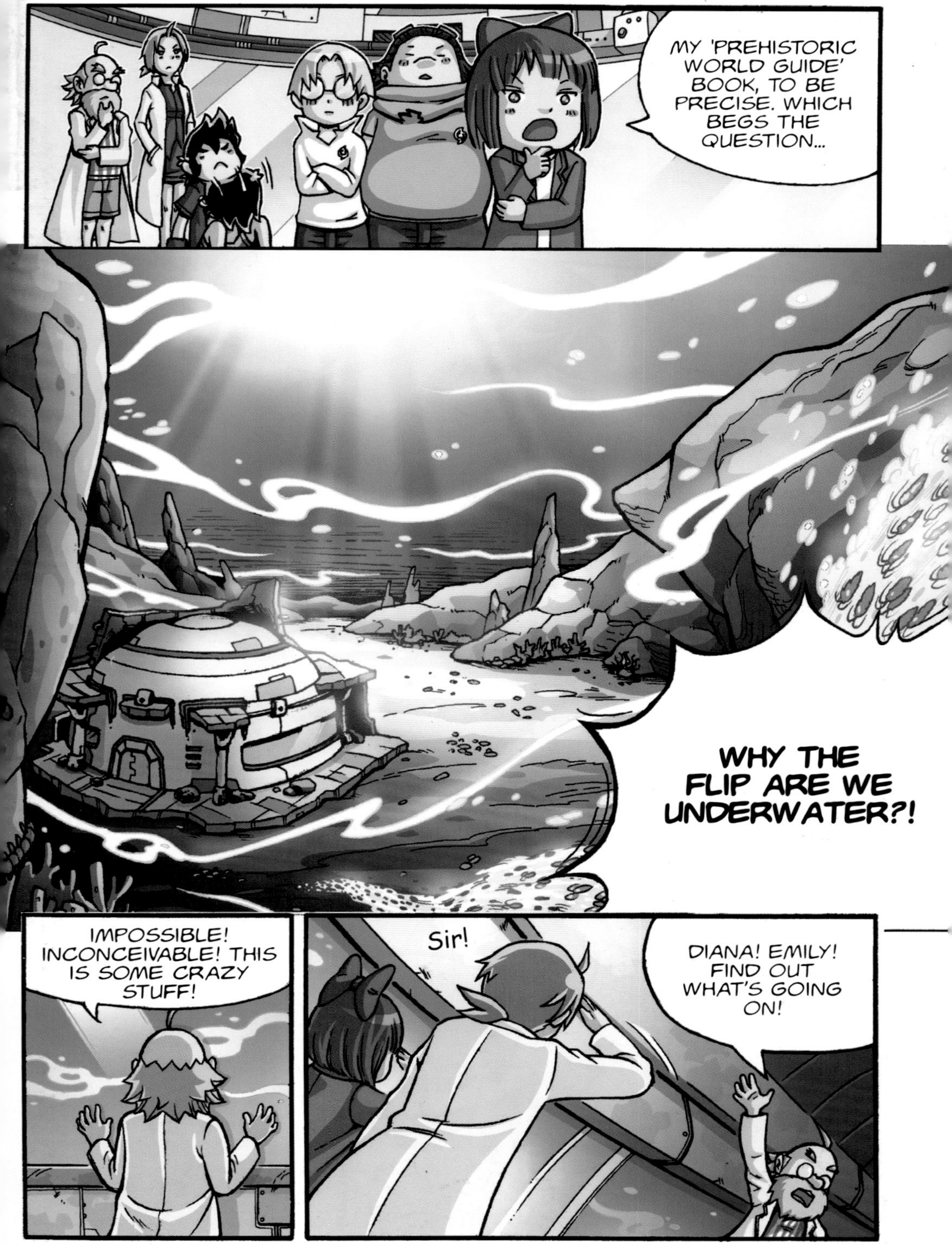
MY 'PREHISTORIC WORLD GUIDE' BOOK, TO BE PRECISE. WHICH BEGS THE QUESTION...
WHY THE FLIP ARE WE UNDERWATER?!
IMPOSSIBLE! INCONCEIVABLE! THIS IS SOME CRAZY STUFF!
Sir!
DIANA! EMILY! FIND OUT WHAT'S GOING ON!

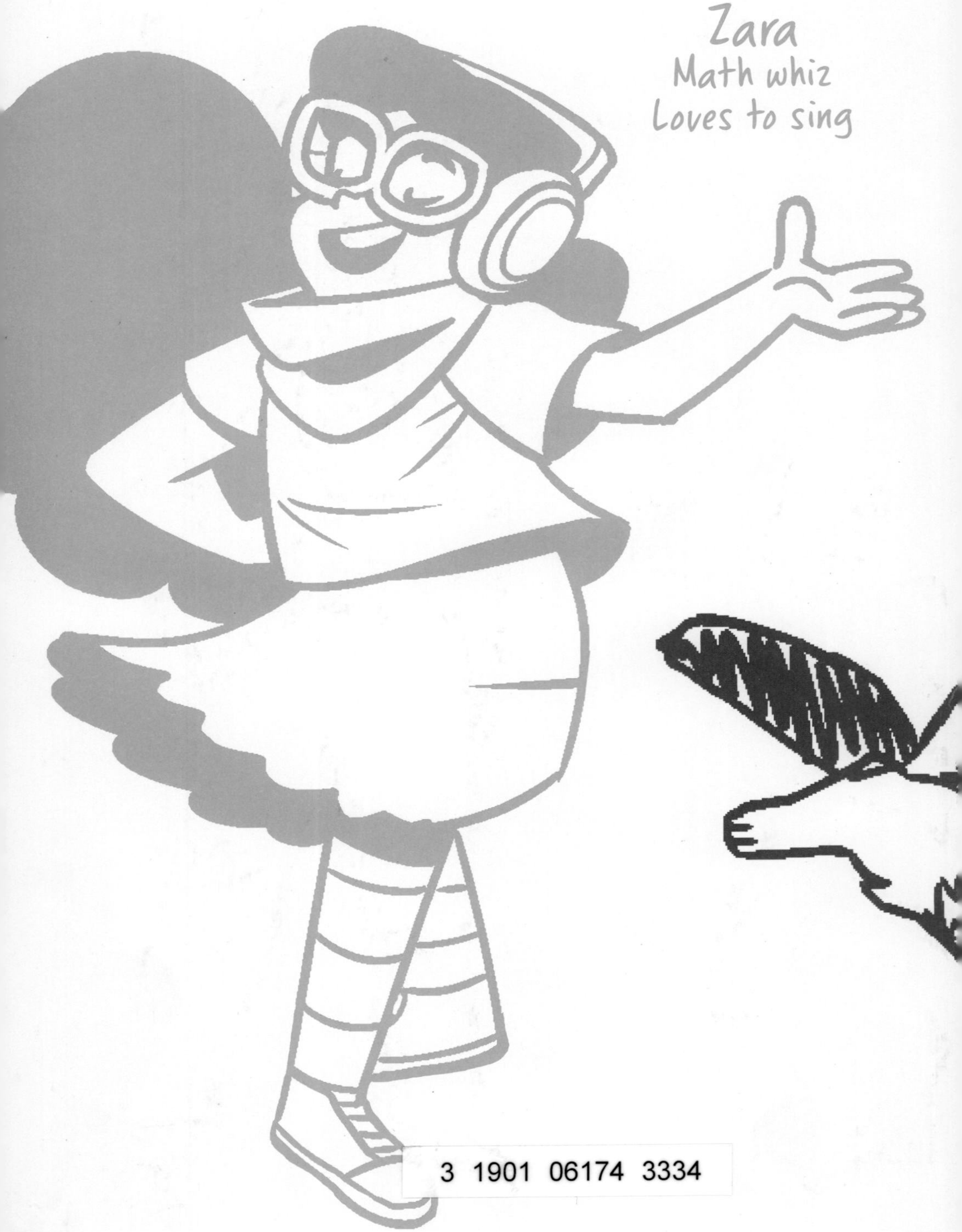
Zara
Math whiz
Loves to sing